ALL
THE
QUEEN'S
SONS

To Avery

ELIZABETH KIPPS

Elizabeth Kipps

ALL THE QUEEN'S SONS

Copyright © 2020 by Elizabeth Kipps

ISBN 9798685708762

Cover Design by Fantastical Ink

Interior Design by Dragonpen Press

*This book is dedicated to Darlene Nelson Stultz
and to the memory of Dale Good Kipps*

CHAPTER ONE

ELEANOR GRACE TWITCHELL was married to Henry Louis Grandin at the age of seventeen. Seventeen is too young for marriage, but girls in Eleanor's day often went through with it anyway. Sometimes this was the result of parental influence or financial necessity. Sometimes it was owing to the girl's own foolish impulse. And sometimes, as in Mrs. Twitchell Grandin's case, it was a dubious medley of all three.

By the time she turned eighteen, young Eleanor had reached the conclusion that marriage was overrated. She felt she'd been robbed of youth's most delectable freedoms and pleasures. Given the chance, she would not have done it over again. She held a firm grip on this conviction for some time, and her nineteenth birthday came and went without loosening her fingers.

But then Eleanor Twitchell Grandin turned twenty. Despite a youthful folly or two, common sense and good judgment had never been terribly far removed from this young lady. Twenty just happened to be when they caught up with her for good.

Now a grown woman, Eleanor looked at her husband one day with the sudden and unshakable comprehension that he was what one would call a *good man*. Henry Louis Grandin worked hard. He acted as a neighbor to everyone he met, regardless of whether they lived down the street or in a different town entirely. With his young wife, he had ever been patient, attentive, and true. The winsome smile and good nature that had first attracted her to him, but then seemed to lose their luster in the humdrum of everyday married life, shone brighter than ever in the light of her other realizations.

The long and short of it is that, at twenty, Eleanor Twitchell Grandin fell headlong in love with her husband. Marriage, she concluded, was not so bad after all. Later that year, she gave birth to their first and only child, a son whom they called Henry Louis Jr.

Around the same time, Mrs. Grandin's husband, a shoe-maker by trade, decided to go into business for himself. Henry Louis Sr. had the good fortune to be offered the purchase of a former employer's shop at a fair price. Because his predecessor had a reputation for being a very lazy shoemaker, it took a year or so for business to blossom. But Grandin painted over the old sign with his own name, and the shop was in a good location, in the part of town frequented by people with the best taste and most money.

Most importantly, Henry Grandin was a good shoemaker. He had an excellent wife, who kept his accounts for him, and a fine son, who showed every promise of being an even better shoemaker than his father. The shop soon flourished, and for a long time the family Grandin was as happy as anyone could wish to be.

When Henry Louis Jr. was seventeen years old, his parents had the shop sign painted over again. Where once it had read *Grandin—Shoemaker*, it now proclaimed *Grandin & Son—Shoemakers*. The customers and neighbors remarked on the change favorably, but their admiration turned to concern within a month. Eleanor Twitchell Grandin and her husband were seen going in and out of Dr. Mack's offices once, then twice, then a third time.

No one knew what the matter was until the day the undertaker's coach was spotted parked beneath Grandin & Son's new sign. The senior Grandin, his neighbors learned, had suffered from what Dr. Mack diagnosed as an incurable affliction of the heart. The illness had been swift, and now Henry Louis Sr. was no more.

Eleanor had never been one to let life get the better of her, even at its lowest points. The passing of her husband naturally marked the lowest depth to which she had yet descended. But such a spirit as hers was bound to rise again eventually. As soon as the worst of her grief had passed, that is precisely what Henry Louis Grandin's widow did. Taking stock of what was left to her—namely her husband's shop, a son she was proud of, and two hands of her own—she rolled up her sleeves and got to work.

The sign above the little shoe-shop did not change again, but from that time on, the Grandin it indicated was Eleanor. Many people expected that the widow Grandin would tire of the business and decide to give it up in favor of remarrying. She was only thirty-seven years old, after all. Her eyes were still as blue and her auburn curls as bouncy as they'd been in her youth. Not a few men in the neighborhood would have been happy to give her a new last name.

Eleanor Twitchell Grandin had other plans.

Under her care, and with the help of her son, the shoe-shop thrived, becoming even more successful than it had been before. There is little that a woman with busy hands and a sharp mind cannot accomplish, and Eleanor was living proof of that.

Mother and son continued in this way for some years, until the latter took a liking to a young lady by the name of Constance Bell. Miss Bell was not a woman of rank or riches, but she had a good heart and good sense. At twenty-five, none could say she was either too young or too old for marriage. Henry Louis Grandin Jr. took the trouble of getting to know Miss Bell better, and she did likewise, and no one was at all surprised when the two fell in love and married.

Eleanor was well pleased with her new daughter-in-law. Her pleasure doubled within the year, as the glowing young couple announced she was to be a grandmother. Alas! More grief tempered the joy of this new arrival. Constance Bell Grandin gave birth to a healthy baby girl but lost her own life in the bargain. She was buried in the family plot, near Henry Louis Sr., and the family Grandin numbered three once again.

Fortunately, tragedy had pretty much done with the Grandins by that time. For a long time, no excitement touched their lives apart from that which a growing child is sure to invite. Verity Grandin had a happy childhood. Because the Grandins' home was located upstairs from their business, she was all but raised in the shoe-shop. Verity delighted in helping her father and grandmother with their work, and she loved her family's shop second only to her family itself.

Through all the additions and subtractions to the household, all the highs and lows, one constant remained. Grandin & Son continued to be among the finest shoemakers in the city, with a reputation that was second to none. The pinnacle of their success came unexpectedly one day when Verity was twelve years old.

A stony-faced, well-dressed man entered the shop and greeted its proprietors with the most formal of bows. In one gloved hand, he held a large, crisp white envelope. Young Verity did not notice this right away. She was preoccupied with the inferiority of his shoes, particularly as they compared with the rest of him. It was, she thought, a good thing he had come. She and her Nonna and father would soon have him properly shod.

But when Verity tore her attention away from the man's feet, she noticed something else, and that *something* snatched every other thought from her head. A patch of embroidered green and gold was sewn to the man's coat, on the left side above his heart. Verity recognized it at once as the insignia of the royal family.

With another bow and a word of greeting, this consequential gentleman presented the envelope he carried to

Eleanor Twitchell Grandin. Verity could scarcely contain her curiosity as Nonna broke the red, impressive-looking wax seal and unfolded the thick paper. Her expression did not change as she read its contents, but her granddaughter saw a spark catch in her eyes.

"Oh, what does it say?" cried Verity. "Tell us, Nonna!"

Eleanor Twitchell Grandin handed the letter to her son before smiling down at Verity. "It is from the queen."

"The *queen*!"

"Yes."

"What has she written us?"

Even the well-dressed gentleman could not prevent a smile from trespassing across his somber countenance. "The queen has learned of your family's excellent reputation, young miss," he said. "She has written to beg admittance to Grandin & Son's list of clientele."

Henry Louis Jr. squeezed his daughter's shoulder. "Remember this day, Verity. It's not just anyone who gets asked to make shoes for royalty."

Faithful to her father's instruction, Verity never did forget that day. But before many years passed, she had come to rue it.

CHAPTER TWO

MUCH LIKE ELEANOR Twitchell Grandin, the Crown Princess Lucerne married when she was seventeen years old. Also much like Eleanor, she soon learned to think ill of the arrangement. In her case, however, duty took precedence over all else. And Lucerne was nothing if not dutiful. If she resented the societal expectations that demanded her advantageous marriage and the loss of girlish liberties, she made no show of it to the public.

Lucerne had been orphaned young, and for years the rule of the land fell to a council of regents. At eighteen, however, Lucerne was legally of age, and on her birthday, she was crowned queen. Not all her subjects were thrilled with the idea of being governed by a teenage girl, and many were abashed to find that her husband did little to assert any authority of his own. Neither of the two enjoyed much popularity, at first.

Public opinion first began to turn in the queen's favor when she gave birth to a male heir. A second son arrived little less than two years later. By that time, Lucerne's subjects had begun to realize that her merits were not limited to the delivery of healthy baby boys. She never wavered in the face of criticism. She showed a gift for discerning good counsel from bad. Her edicts proved to be wise and just. She made no grand displays of wealth or power.

Approval for Lucerne's rule increased as steadily as her family did. Following the Princes Augustin and Christopher came the Princes Marcus, Alexander, Cassiel, and Demetris. The queen's husband died shortly after the arrival of their sixth son, a loss her people mourned dutifully. They dressed in their most somber shades and made daily remarks about the misfortune. Within a few weeks, however, their grief had run its course. Blacks and grays were relegated once more to the backs of the kingdom's wardrobes, and conversation returned to subjects less grim.

As well it might. The kingdom was a picture of prosperity by that time. Lucerne had ushered in what her subjects began to call a golden age. With their queen in her prime, not to mention plenty of princes for their future security, the people knew the sun was shining upon them.

All sun-basking societies are sure to have a thing or two in common, one of which is soil rich for cultivating gossip. Naturally, the thing Lucerne's subjects delighted in discussing more than any other was the royal family. The queen herself was too revered to generate much tattle. Occasionally, someone might try to spark a rumor that she intended to remarry, but such tales were never grounded enough to gain momentum. The queen's sons provided far more tantalizing fodder.

Though the population generally agreed that they were exceptional youths, with perfect manners, superior intelligence, and charming appearance, the truth was that no one had any way of knowing for sure. Few had had occasion to glimpse them in the flesh, and fewer still could boast of having met them. Most who had did not relish the honor for long, as curious acquaintances sprang from the woodwork to hound them with questions. One woman who had served as a governess to the younger children faced such zealous inquisitions from her neighbors that she was obliged to relocate and change her name.

The older the princes grew, the more they intrigued the populace at large. Some gossips began to say that perhaps they were not such model princes after all. If the queen kept them shut away, she must have a reason for it, and the likeliest reason was that they were horrid, ungrateful little brats who were not fit to be seen.

If such tales gave Lucerne any trepidation, she made no display of it. She certainly did not speak of it, to her boys or to anyone else. As far as she was concerned, her family's private life was closed for public viewing.

The queen had particular ideas about what young men ought to be. Exposure to the influences of fame and popular society could only thwart such ideals, so she did all she could to bring her boys up in quiet and privacy.

But while fictions created by the public were no more provoking to the queen than a fistful of feathers hurled in her direction, the truth of the princes' conduct brought her no end of headache. To be sure, they were all of them clever enough to behave in her presence. The trouble was that, most of the time, they were *not* in her presence. She had a country to run, as well as a family to raise. Much of the day-to-day care for her sons had to be entrusted to tutors and governesses.

For everyone but these select men and women, employment in the palace was regarded as a great honor. If the housekeeper had to tell Lucerne about a maid misplacing some of the silver, it was but a trifle. If her equerry brought her news that one of her best horses had been lamed, he did so without fear. If land agents were forced to acknowledge that their plans had failed in one way or another, they knew to expect mercy. But if one of the six princes happened to fall and sprain a wrist or put up a poor showing in his mathematics or get caught napping in the library, the very portraits on the wall seemed to tremble.

It was only natural that the queen should value her sons more than her silver, horses, or land. None close to her could speak against her concern for their welfare. Not even the tutors and governesses themselves dared protest. How could they? She only wanted what was best for her children, like any mother would. Still, to be caught between six mischievous princes and the queen's steely maternal backbone was not a condition anyone relished or envied.

Chief among Lucerne's staff and advisers was Sir Rufus, a lean gentleman of middling years. When concerns related to the princes happened to arise, Sir Rufus was almost always entreated to take it to the queen. This was due to the lamentable fact that he was her brother-in-law and the boys' uncle.

One fateful afternoon, a matter was brought to Sir Rufus's attention that disturbed him exceedingly. He was an easily disturbed man, Sir Rufus. Thoughts of germs, war-hungry neighboring kings, and potential barley crop failures often kept him awake at night. But this bit of intelligence would have troubled him even if he had not been naturally given to worrying. The royal treasurer, a man who usually had the nerves of a brigadier general and a countenance to match, had been pale as birch bark when he delivered it. Sir Rufus fretted for a while, trying to make sense of the thing. But the more one puts off an undesirable task, the more dreadful it will become. Sir Rufus steeled himself, going to the queen as soon as it was convenient for her to see him.

He met her in her private study, where she sat behind a desk, finishing a letter. Though Lucerne was an attractive woman, her late husband had been the last person to remark on it. She gave no thought to her own appearance and dressed as simply as any common widow. No one thought to compliment the thick waves and unyielding darkness of her hair, given that she wore it cropped. Such was far from the popular style amongst ladies at the time, and if she hadn't been such a respected ruler, people would have called it shocking.

Apart from her unusual choice of hairstyle, one aspect of the queen's appearance was impossible to overlook, and that was her eyes. They were round and deep and piercing. They looked as if they saw into everything, but one could not quite see into *them*. It was like staring out the window of a lighted room in the dark of night.

Under the enigmatic gaze of these eyes, Sir Rufus bowed and cleared his throat.

"Rufus," said Queen Lucerne. "Tell me what is on your mind."

"Well...there is a rather troubling matter we feel must be brought to your attention."

"Regarding?"

"Well, Your Grace, it pertains to"—here Rufus paused to evict yet another frog from his throat—"your sons."

The queen sighed. "Which one?"

"Er, well, *all* of them, I suppose."

"And what have they done this time?"

"I know of no particular offense, your grace," Rufus said, struggling to come to the point. "It's only something, shall I say, *odd* that Mr. Banks brought to my attention this morning."

The queen folded her hands on her lap and continued with no outward demonstration of impatience. "What did my treasurer have to say about my children?"

"It seems that there have been some—ah—*extravagances* where the boys are concerned. Quite a bit of silver has disappeared over the past months, and...er—"

"They have been stealing?"

"No! Nothing so terrible. Of course not! The fact is that a most shocking sum has been spent on their—well, on their *shoes*."

"*Shoes?*" repeated the queen.

"Yes, *shoes*, Your Grace."

"I don't believe it possible for six boys, even growing ones, to dent the royal treasury for nothing but shoes. I recollect that the tradesman who supplies us is a fair one."

"The Grandins are the very best sort of family, to be sure. But with such quantities as have been required, why—"

"What do you mean, *quantities*?"

"The princes are going through a pair or more of shoes in a fortnight, Your Grace. A pair apiece."

"That is preposterous. There must be some mistake."

Sir Rufus had a fat sheaf of bills at the ready. He watched as the queen quietly examined them. At length, she furrowed her brow and called for a servant.

"Please go to my sons' quarters and fetch me back a pair of shoes."

"A particular pair?" asked the conscientious servant.

"No, any will do."

When the shoes arrived, she took one while Sir Rufus examined the other. Judging from the neat, embossed script on the inner tongue, they belonged to Cassiel, the fifth-born prince.

"Why, they must be hiding a pet!" declared Rufus, indicating the nicked, discolored leather. "This looks like nothing if not the doings of a mischievous dog."

Lucerne pinched the shoe's outer sole, which flapped free of its heel. "You do my Cassiel too little credit," she said. "He is quite mischievous enough to have done this on his own."

"Yes, and I don't suppose a dog would have made off with the entire insole," Rufus added, peering inside the shoe.

"This was good leather. The fault isn't with the craftsmanship. I've never had the hint of a problem with my own shoes. You say the other boys' are just as bad?"

"From what I gather."

"How can you explain it, Rufus?"

"I simply cannot, Your Grace. It is a mystery."

"What of Augustin? You are with him every day." The queen referred to her eldest and heir. Since completing his primary education some months prior, he had been transferred to the tutelage of Rufus and several of her trusted ministers. "Perhaps he has betrayed something that might help explain."

Rufus shook his head. "No, Your Grace, nothing. Augustin never lets a word out without thinking twice and thrice before he says it. Would you have me question him on the matter?"

"No, Rufus. That won't do."

"All the boys together, then? I will send for them this moment, if you give me the word."

Lucerne traced the shape of her chin between her thumb and forefinger. The wrinkle between her brows deepened, and she shook her head. "You know as well as I do that if they *are* up to no good, they'll be the last ones to own it."

Rufus had nothing left to clear from his throat by this time, but that didn't prevent his trying. "Perhaps—" he started to say, then fumbled. He could think of no way to voice his true thoughts and settled for a feeble shrug instead. "Boys will be boys, Your Grace."

"These are not just any boys...they are mine," said the queen. After a moment of fragile silence, she lifted her chin. "You shall simply have to help me watch them more closely."

"Me?" Rufus squeaked.

"Yes. We must enlist only a trustworthy few...my house-keeper and steward, the chief of guards...the boys' tutors, to be sure. Someone will see something, Rufus. I'll have an answer by the end of the week, and we'll put this nonsense behind us."

CHAPTER THREE

ABOVE THE FRONT door inside the Grandins' shoe shop, a small bell hung from a tarnished brass curlicue. Whenever someone went in or out, the bell proclaimed it with pomp and cheer. Verity Grandin had known the sound from infancy. She grew up cherishing it with the kind of love that is not conscious of loving; the kind one isn't aware of until the object is taken away.

When the Grandins were first appointed official shoe-makers to the royal family, excitement had reigned both in their own home and in the neighborhood around them. Everyone wanted to buy their shoes from the queen's own supplier. Lately, however, the demand had grown to be too much, even with Verity helping. In order to meet the needs of the queen's sons and maintain their usual quality, the Grandins were forced to turn away many of their other customers, even some of the oldest and most loyal among them.

Thus, while Grandin & Son remained the best shoemakers in the city and were paid well for their toil, much of the joy had gone from their shop. The bell at the door had been all but silent for months.

If the mother and son resented their lot, they never gave voice to it. But Verity knew them well enough to read the sadness in their silence, and their grief found a home in her own heart. The family had success and renown, but it had come at the cost of their former cheer and contentment. For this, they had the queen's sons to thank.

"I never knew boys could hoard shoes the way these do," she complained to her father one day. "And I can't understand why a queen as good as ours puts up with it."

She was polishing one of said shoes at the moment, freshly crafted for the young Prince Demetris. Morning sunlight beamed on her back and dappled the floor with shadows of the finished shoes that were strung up in the window.

The rest of the shop would have presented a jumbled picture to the untrained eye. A long workbench running parallel to one wall was littered with pegs, paring and skiving knives, awls, trenchets, blocks, and hammers. Shelves overflowed with jars of paste and polish, spools of thread, and chunks of papered wax. Lasts and stirrups dangled from another wall. Regardless of appearances, everything in the shop was systemized, from the crooked stacks of uncut leather to the smallest tack.

Unlike some shoemakers' workshops, no newfangled machinery glinted within the Grandins' walls. Eleanor Twitchell Grandin had recently noted that such advancements would not be beyond their means. But Henry Jr. insisted on making every cut and stitch with his own two hands, using the quality tools he knew he could rely upon.

On this morning, he was putting the finishing touches on a shoe for Augustin, the eldest prince, who had narrow feet with high arches that presented a special challenge.

"I'm not aware our shoes are being hoarded," he told his daughter. "It seems they're roughly used, is all. The man brought a pair for me to see not two weeks ago, and they were worn to shreds."

Verity continued her own task with increasing vigor. "Well, I think it's disgraceful that anyone should ruin a pair of *our* shoes as quickly as these princes do. They must be horrible."

"It's our business to make the shoes, Verity. What people do with them after they're bought and paid for is their concern."

"Still, if I were you, I'm sure I'd give them a piece of my mind, the next I saw them."

Her father had been invited to the palace several times for the purpose of measuring and remeasuring the young men's growing feet. He was not a man of many words and had never troubled himself to give much description of the queen's sons. He assured his family that, apart from such peculiarities as Prince Augustin's arches, there was little to tell. But now, he grew thoughtful.

"The gossips might say they're wild boys," he said, "but if they are, they're very good at hiding it. Such odd characters! Like soldiers, or automatons. I've never seen a smile or a snicker. Not one has ever so much as spoken out of turn." He paused, sighing. "In any event, they are the sons of our queen, and they are customers. We must treat them with respect."

Verity pursed her lips. Whatever their reasons, the queen's sons were scandalously good at spoiling their shoes. She would not forgive them for it. But she loved her father too well to argue against the things he said, and so she pursued the subject no further.

Later that same day, Verity made the short walk to the neighborhood bakery. By some merry quirk of providence, the baker's name happened to be Baker. His shop had an enormous window for displaying all of his various loaves and dainties, along with a sign painted in friendly red and gold. Everything inside was clean and white. The walls were white, the paper bags that Mrs. Baker handed to customers over the counter were white, Mr. Baker's floppy hat was white, and his white apron was always dusted with generous amounts of white flour. The only contrast was in the rosy glow of Mr. Baker's plump cheeks.

Baker's was always busy, and this day was no exception. Verity slipped inside, inhaling deeply, for she loved the scent of fresh baked bread. She took her place at the end of the queue, behind two girls her own age. They both wore dresses that were too grown up for them, with silk ribbons in their hair and white gloves on their hands. They looked like girls who were used to being complimented by everyone they met.

Verity had never gotten that kind of attention. No one could call her pretty and really mean it, or so she believed. Of course, Nonna made some mention of Verity's beauty every other day. But Nonna didn't count. Verity had known the truth since the summer she turned nine years old. Two women had entered the shop one day and, after critiquing some shoes, proceeded to comment upon her person as if she were just another slipper in the window.

"I say," one had begun. "Look at that poor little creature."

"I wonder how old she is? Her figure isn't a bit promising. And she's frightfully pale."

"Perhaps she suffers from indifferent health."

"It must be so! Poor child. Her hair is a most unfortunate shade."

"Freckles, too! I don't envy her parents when the time comes to find a husband for her."

Both the women were tall and well-formed, with smooth skin, delicate hands, and golden hair. They were pictures of classic beauty, and Verity had no reason to believe that they didn't know what they were talking about. Even though she had grown into more of a young lady by now, she was still freckle-faced, redheaded, and snub-nosed. The women's words when she was nine still held true today.

Verity tried not to let it bother her, instead adopting the belief that there were more important things in the world than being attractive. This was true, of course, and she might have embraced many a worse ideal. Yet while being pretty is of small import in the grand scheme of things, it is a good thing for a girl to feel so every now and then. And a girl who *feels* pretty is much more likely to *look* it, anyway.

Verity turned her face from the girls in the bakery, back toward the window. Unfortunately, she could do nothing to block out their conversation.

"Well, I met Rose Figg in Ashforth Street yesterday, and she had seen them, too," one of the girls was saying in a tone she seemed to think was a whisper but emphatically was not. "Just on the other side of the palace gate!"

"Rose? Indeed! Which did *she* say had the most pleasing looks?"

"Oh, Prince Marcus, to be sure. There can be no two opinions on the matter. The boy has eyelashes any woman would kill for, Virne. And *such* a chin!"

"You couldn't really have seen him close enough to judge his eyelashes, Clementina?"

"Of course I could!" Clementina said. "And I was especially careful to take note of them. For *your* benefit, not my own. Really, Virne, I thought you'd be more grateful."

"I am, Clementina, I am! Do go on. I want to hear it all."

"Well, as I was saying...Prince Marcus is easily the handsomest. It's when deciding who is second and third that things get difficult."

As soon as she realized what the girls were talking about, Verity silently cursed her luck. She'd have been less repelled to hear a couple of old men comparing notes on their intestinal complaints. She was tempted to put her fingers in her ears as the two babbled on, and probably would have done it if it wouldn't have attracted attention.

"What do you mean, Clementina?"

"Well, Prince Alexander is nothing at all to look at. And then there are Demetris and Cassiel. They are too young to think of yet. Prince Demetris is but ten years old, you know. He does have promise, though, Virne, and I daresay our little sisters will be wild for him in a few years. It is Augustin and Christopher that give us trouble. I say *us*, dear, because Rose Figg felt just the same as I do."

"Tell me, Clementina!"

"I'm *trying*, Virne. You see, Christopher has a lovely wave in his hair and dimples. But his mouth is all askew, and it quite ruins the rest of his features."

"And Prince Augustin?"

"He's the tallest, and his hair is a little darker than the others. All of them wear it short, Virne, and parted on the side. It's terribly old-fashioned, but really charming, when you see it on *them.* Anyway, Augustin has fine features. His nose is nearly perfect. The trouble is, he looked as if he were on his way to a funeral."

"Perhaps you spotted him in a dull moment."

"Oh, no. When one wears a face like that, it is almost always because one practices it. And besides, Rose said he looked just the same to her."

"So, which is better looking, Clementina? Prince Augustin or Prince Christopher?"

"I shall tell you first thing, when I reach a conclusion on the matter."

Verity offered a prayer of silent thanksgiving as Mr. Baker called upon the girls to serve them. They paid for their confections, and the last Verity heard of them was Clementina exclaiming about her friend opening her parasol before they were in the street.

"What can I get for you today, Miss Grandin?" asked Mr. Baker, as he waved her forward.

"Just a loaf of the flaxseed, please."

He took the bread from a shelf behind the counter and wrapped it in white paper, looking at her with a twinkle in his eye. "Are you sure I can't interest you in some plum cake, as well? It's very good today!"

"I'm sure it is, Mr. Baker," she said, returning his smile.

"Just a slice, perhaps? Or would you prefer a gingersnap? Mrs. Baker just took them out of the oven."

"No, thank you. Just the loaf today."

"My sweets will never match up to your grandmama's, will they?" Mr. Baker smiled, taking the coins that she handed him. "You tell her I said hello. And your father, too."

"I certainly will. Thank you."

Verity headed back into the sunny street and made her way to Miss Dancer's cheese shop, then finally to the chemist to pick up a prescription for Nonna. On her way home, she had to stop to free a bothersome pebble from her shoe.

"*Verity Grandin*," said someone behind her, just as she straightened up and rearranged the packages in her arms.

Verity had no desire to meet the young man who belonged to this particular voice. She grimaced. Then she made the mistake of glancing backward, which he took as an invitation to join her. After that, it was too late to do anything but walk a little faster and look straight ahead.

"Oi, shop girl! Since when did you get too high and mighty to greet your own neighbors?"

"Good morning, Erik. There, I've greeted you. Are you satisfied?"

"Let me buy you some pear drops, and that'll do me." Erik grinned, gesturing at a sweets shop across the road.

"No, thank you."

"What about some licorice whips?"

"I'd rather chew on my father's shoe leather. Now, if you don't mind—"

"At least let me carry your packages for you. They look heavy."

"They're not. And even if they were, I could manage them just fine."

"You're the snippiest little miss what ever was, Grandin. I don't see anyone else paying you attention. You ought to be grateful to me for noticing you."

"Is there any female person under the age of twenty-five that you *don't* notice?"

"I only have eyes for you, shop girl."

"If that's the case, Erik Burns, then I hope a catbird comes along and pecks them out."

She picked up her pace to an all-out trot. Combined with her last retort, this was enough to dissuade young Burns from continuing at her side. But he was too proud not to have a last word, and he shouted after her loud enough for half the street to hear.

"What are you waiting for? A prince to come along and sweep you off your feet?"

Her cheeks burning with indignation, Verity whirled to glare at Erik. "If a prince did come," she said, "I'd knock him off his feet before I gave him the chance to sweep me off mine!"

This silenced Erik at last, and Verity turned for home.

Couldn't the princes leave even the smallest part of her life untouched? They haunted her home. They lay in wait to ambush her in every corner of her own neighborhood.

Walking past the building that had once been her school, she sighed. The princes had even gone so far as to chase her from its familiar halls. Her education—her entire life—was on hold while she helped her father and Nonna keep up with their work. The work of making shoes for the princes.

Verity glanced back several times before reaching her own front door, as if expecting to find her steps dogged by the queen's sons. Though no one with a crown on his head and her father's shoes on his feet appeared, Verity couldn't be rid of the feeling that she had six royal shadows. And the weight on her heart pressed all the heavier.

CHAPTER FOUR

THE SIX PRINCES took breakfast with their mother each Sunday and supped with her on Mondays, Wednesdays, Fridays, and alternating Saturdays. She was known to look in on their studies once or twice a week, but apart from that, the routine never changed. Thus, the boys were taken unawares when, one Tuesday morning, just as they'd begun to pitch into their toast and eggs, Lucerne appeared in the breakfast room. Chewing stopped, forks were dropped, and the boys hurried to their feet as their mother seated herself at the head of the table.

"As you were," she said, and they resumed their seats. The queen poured herself a cup of tea. "How quiet you are all of a sudden! Augustin, is something the matter?"

The eldest prince straightened his spine, held back his shoulders, and tried to encounter her gaze without looking into her eyes. "No, Your Grace."

"Christopher?"

"We might be wondering what you're doing here, is all, Your Grace."

"Why shouldn't I be here? This is my home, isn't it? And you are my children, the last I checked."

"But it's Tuesday!" proclaimed a young voice from the table's foot.

"What difference ought that to make, Cassiel?"

"I don't know."

"Then perhaps you'd have been wiser to hold your tongue. Alexander? You're yawning."

"Excuse me, Your Grace."

"Didn't you sleep well?"

"Quite well, thank you."

"Tell me what time you went to bed."

Alexander flushed. His mouth parted, but no voice came out. One of his brothers swooped in.

"Sandy turns in at the same time as the rest of us, of course. In bed at nine thirty, lights out at quarter to ten. Just like always."

"Thank you, Christopher, but I prefer my questions answered by those to whom they are put. Alexander?"

"It was just like Christy says. Just like always."

"Are you *quite* certain?"

Her persistence alarmed Alexander out of speech. Indeed, it worried all of the princes. The youngest of them was a stout lad, however, and recovering himself speedily, he raised his hand.

"What is it, Demetris?"

"They're lying, Your Grace."

Prince Marcus was best poised to kick the traitor from under the table and did not hesitate to do so. Demetris didn't flinch but answered boldly when Lucerne bade him continue. "Sometimes," he said, "Sandy stays up after the lights are put out and reads."

"How does he manage it with no light?" the queen wondered.

Demetris bit his lip, but Cassiel intervened.

"He sits by the window. Only when there's a moon out. It was full last night, so it's no wonder he's tired this morning."

The queen pushed away her cup and stood. Alexander's cheeks were pinker than the roses on the tea set.

"You have plenty of time to read while the sun is up, Alexander. I don't want you ruining your eyesight."

"Yes, Your Grace."

"Is there anything else any of you want to tell me?"

Her question was answered with silence and shaking heads.

"Very well. Best finish your breakfast or you won't be on time for your lessons. Mr. Hawk and Miss Clement tell me that you've been tardy several mornings these past few weeks. It is very discourteous to be late. You all know better."

"Yes, Your Grace," they replied in chorus.

Lucerne's troubled gaze lingered momentarily on her boys before she slipped back through the door. Six sighs of relief followed her out.

"I thought she was onto us!" declared the youngest. "Sorry to throw you to the dogs like that, Sandy."

"That's alright, Tris. I should thank you. All those questions scared the wits out of me."

"We could see that," sassed Marcus, his mouth full of toast. Christopher threw a balled-up napkin at him.

"Shut up, Goose."

"Don't call me Goose! You know I can't stand it. And the rest of you all get normal nicknames. It isn't fair!"

"Maybe if you quit honking about it all the time, we'd forget the likeness," Christy said with a wry quirk of his brow.

"Yeah!" added Cal. "Then we could come up with something even better. Like *Marcie*."

"Or *Cuss*," Tris suggested, sniggering.

Marcus scowled and started to make further protest, but Augustin cut him off.

"Isn't anyone else even a little worried?"

"What about?" huffed Goose, his feathers still ruffled.

"The queen, obviously. You kids might be proud enough of that excuse you invented, but she won't be fooled for long, if she is at all——"

He was interrupted as a maid came in to clear away their dirty dishes. After she'd gone, he resumed in a whisper.

"Maybe we haven't been as careful as we think. Maybe we had better cut it out, while we still can. I don't like all these risks and secrets, Christy."

Christopher leaned back in his chair. All eyes were on him.

"Well, it's whatever you boys want to do. If it's getting to be too much for you, we can quit any time. Go back to life the way it was before. Be discreet and decent. No more adventure."

"And no dancing," added Marcus.

"Or company," put in Cassiel.

"Or fun," sighed Demetris.

"It's risky," murmured Alexander, "but I still think it's worth it."

"Well, Augie?" Christopher asked, looking at their eldest brother, whose arms were crossed.

"I'll be the one whose goose is cooked, if we get caught."

"You know we'd never let that happen. It's us versus the queen. If we go down, we do it together. Right, boys?"

A chorus of agreement followed, and Augustin was forced to relinquish his protest.

Sir Rufus paced from one end of the room to the other. Queen Lucerne sat behind her desk, eyes cast downward. A fortnight of heightened observations had not unveiled a solution to their riddle. No one had seen anything out of the ordinary in the princes' behavior. They took their meals and attended to their lessons, just the same as ever. The only conclusion Lucerne could draw was that, however the boys were spoiling their shoes, they were doing it after dark. This disturbed her all the more.

"But if it's really so important," the exasperated Rufus was saying, "then why *can't* you just put guards inside their rooms?"

"I want a *cure* for the problem," the queen replied. "Not a mere tourniquet."

"Then supposing you were to split the boys up? Put them all in different rooms."

"Isolate them? Rufus, you know how attached they are to one another. When Augustin had to leave lessons with his brothers to begin his further education, you'd have thought there was a death in the family."

"I cannot deny it. The poor lad still behaves as if he's in mourning."

"Exactly. Too much more upheaval, and we'll have an all-out rebellion on our hands. I won't risk it. You know that it is crucial we keep this business quiet."

"But surely there must be *something*—"

"Sir Rufus," interrupted Lucerne. "I want to know *what* my sons are up to. But I must also know *why*. You must pull weeds out by the root, if you don't want them to grow back. And you must dig to the root of a problem if you don't want more problems to breed."

"Does this mean you plan to actually confront the boys about it?"

The queen smoothed her skirts. The muscles in her neck tightened, and she had to swallow and moisten her lips before answering. "I've given them every opportunity to confess. But I can see the raptures of a shared secret in their faces. No...a direct confrontation will be of no use."

"What, then?"

"Do you remember Charles Gandil?"

"The old spy? He's been retired for years and living off a fat pension in Upper Windbough, if I'm not mistaken."

"I want you to send for him. And Frederick Merkle and Harold Chase. Be as discreet as you can about it, but I want to see them all here. Together."

"You want to invite your best spy and detectives to the palace. At the same time. Immediately. And in secret."

"Yes."

Rufus frowned, but nodded. The queen bowed her own head. She did not like the plan any more than he did. But what choice did she have? Her sons would not confide in her. Their boyish mischief—whatever it was—had already resulted in lies and secrets. Things would only get worse if she did not act now.

The princes had to be uprooted. It was for their own good.

CHAPTER FIVE

VERITY GRANDIN LIKED to wake up with the sun. The birds outside her window served in place of an alarm clock. As soon as she had blinked the sleep from her eyes, she was up and pulling the curtains aside, eager to have a look at the morning. It seemed to her that she could always judge the sort of day it was going to be, just by greeting it before either of them had quite gotten going. Once that was taken care of, she could proceed to dress and arrange her hair. She never thought of going to breakfast first. To Verity, breakfast was not only the most important meal of the day, it was the best. She felt bound to treat it with reverence.

This morning, she wandered into the kitchen in such good time that neither her father nor her grandmother had stirred from their rooms yet. The only other soul in the house was the Grandins' part-time maid. Verity found her whisking a bowl of eggs and yawning. A book lay open in front of her, but it did not look like a recipe book. Verity inched up behind the maid to see.

"Are you reading fairy tales, Olive?" she asked.

Liquid egg sloshed out of the bowl as Olive gasped. "You startled me, Miss Grandin!"

Verity smiled by way of an apology and gestured at the maid's book again.

"Begging your pardon, Miss Grandin. I can't deny it's a fairy tale. And it's such a good one I couldn't put it down."

"A children's story?"

"To be sure. Didn't you ever like reading stories, miss?"

"They suited well enough when I was a little girl. Naturally, I grew out of them quite a while ago."

Olive put a ribbon in the book to mark her place, then set it aside. She poured the eggs into a hot skillet and looked thoughtful as specks of grease leaped up in a steamy hiss like fizzling fireworks.

"Well," she said, "people do grow out of fairy tales. But they grow back into them just as often as not."

Verity rolled her eyes, but she didn't let the maid see, and instead of arguing, she helped lay the table for breakfast.

Later that morning, whilst the family was all at work downstairs in the shop, the bell over the door announced a visitor. Verity was disappointed to see that it was only a certain roving leather merchant. Her father was more pleased, as he had need of new sole leather. But his smile vanished when he saw what the man had to offer.

"These are slim pickings, sir," sniffed Nonna to the vendor as she looked over his goods. Unable to defend them, the merchant only crossed his arms and held his nose in the air.

"I can't use any of this." Henry Louis Grandin frowned. "Look here, some of it is damaged. These hides have not been tanned properly. Even if I could make them into shoes, they would not be fit to wear. See how someone has applied blacking here? It comes off on my hands!"

His mother exclaimed again, and the merchant protested that it was not his fault. Verity would have been amused if not for her father's disheartened expression. Their visitor took his leave, promising to come back in a week or so.

"You needn't bother if you don't have better goods by then," muttered Nonna.

Verity's father shook his head. "I have always been able to arrange fair prices with that man when his stock *is* satisfactory. If only that was a more common occurrence! I wanted new sole leather for the next batch of the princes' shoes."

Verity did everything she could to lift her father's spirits. She cleaned his instruments for him, swept the floor, and organized two jars of tacks that had fallen to the floor and gotten jumbled. She chattered all the while about ordinary, agreeable things.

"Thank you, Verity," he told her with a smile at the day's end. "You are a better daughter than any man could deserve. What would I do without you?"

But Verity still sensed that her father was burdened by his responsibilities, and she carried a burden of her own on his behalf.

Her mind was thus weighted as she ventured into the outskirts of town on an errand the next morning. Having been raised in the city, the ordinary sounds of hustle and bustle in the streets were nothing to Verity. But something lurking beneath the ordinary stopped her short in a certain neighborhood.

What is that sound?

Happy to be distracted from her own problems, Verity wandered toward it. The resonance of voices grew more distinct. There were several, and she did not like them. They were harsh and shrill.

She looked about her, glimpsing no signs of a disturbance on the street. But a narrow alley opened to her left not far ahead and Verity had her sights on it in a twinkling. She picked up her feet and rushed forward. Four boys stood near the mouth of the alley, jeering and hurling pebbles at something. At first, Verity took their quarry for a feral dog, and was angered enough. When a closer look revealed it to be a person—and an elderly one, at that!—she all but cried out in her fury. Marching up to the youths, she slapped a stone from the hand of the first one she met. All four stopped to gape at her.

"Of all the wicked things to do!" she said. "You should be ashamed of yourselves!"

The boy she'd struck was red in the face. He was about fifteen years old, the same as Verity, but half a head taller and wiry.

"Hook it!" he snapped. "It's none of your business."

He gave her a cautionary push. Almost as a reflex, Verity slapped him again, this time square across the face. He staggered back with a whimper.

"*You* hook it, or I'll put you on your back!"

The youths mumbled amongst themselves, then shuffled out of the alley one by one. Not until they were gone did

Verity notice her trembling hands. She'd never scrapped with anyone in her life, much less a gang of four. She breathed to calm herself and turned to their victim.

"Are you all right?" she asked, leaning forward with her hands on her knees.

The figure righted itself, and Verity found herself looking into the round, wrinkled face of an elderly woman. She was scarcely larger than a child, and the merry, toothless smile stretched over her mouth took Verity off guard. Her clothes were worn to threads, and though they must once have been dyed in vibrant colors, they'd faded beyond recognition.

"Quite all right!" the woman said. "Thank you, my dear! Yes, thank you very much. You're a plucky lass to stand up for an old lady like that."

"It was nothing," said Verity through a modest blush. "I hope they didn't hurt you."

"A few new bruises, perhaps. I'm none the worse for them."

"Can I help you home? Those rascals went off, but they might come back."

"I come from over the river. I shan't trouble you to go so far, child. But I would be glad of an arm to help me as far as the crossing."

Verity offered the woman her elbow, and they left the alley together. She was further startled by her companion's lively step.

"What horrible boys those were," she remarked. A scowl returned to taint her lips, but the woman let out a cheerful bark of a laugh.

"They thought I was a witch, the silly things! Perhaps they were more frightened than horrible. You saw how ready they were to scamper away. People will do such foolish things when they are afraid."

"Maybe, but I'm sure I'd be more upset about it, if I were you."

"When you're as old as I am, you learn not to hold too tightly. It's no use fretting about things, especially once they're over and done with."

Verity walked on, looking straight ahead. She could not persuade her own thoughts to be quite so generous as those of this woman.

"You have a firm grip, young miss!"

"Oh! I'm so sorry."

"You needn't be. But if you clasp your fists as tightly as that, the fingers will start to grow into your palm. What troubles are you clinging to?"

Verity flushed. "It's nothing. I was still thinking of those boys, is all."

"Is that so?" The woman spoke as if she knew very well it wasn't, which unnerved Verity. It was one thing to help someone in need, quite another to share her own problems with a stranger. But the woman seemed to understand even this. "I'm just an old dotard," she said, smiling again. "Of course you must hold your tongue, if you think it right. Just see that you don't swallow it, my dear."

They strolled by a handsome brick building with an impressive gilt placard that read *Frederick Merkle, Detective*.

"My, my!" the old woman remarked. "It seems Mr. Merkle cannot be bothered to keep his stair swept anymore.

And look! Do you see how his windows are left shrouded, even at this hour?"

"How peculiar," Verity said. "I thought Frederick Merkle was supposed to be a great sleuth, but his house looks as if it wants to be left alone."

"Well put," the woman chuckled. "Mr. Merkle has shut himself in. And Mr. Chase's offices on the other side of town are in a similar state."

"But why?"

"I expect they're proud men and can't bear that they finally encountered a case they couldn't solve. Even a humble man might sulk to be sent away by the queen!"

"Oh yes," Verity agreed. "I'd rather die than feel I failed queen and country. But what would our queen want with detectives? I've heard nothing of this."

"Few have! Or will. The queen would not like for the public to think that she hasn't got the same firm hold on her own children as she does on her country."

"Is it about those princes, then? Well, I'm not surprised. I'm sure they must be little monsters, the way they go through their shoes."

"Ah!" the little woman cried. "You know more than you think. Girls your age often do."

"What do you mean?"

"All the queen's sons have such a talent for spoiling their shoes, and no one can tell why. Not even the greatest detectives!"

Curiosity and resentment swelled in Verity's chest like an ocean wave. "Is Queen Lucerne really worried about the shoes?"

"To be sure, child! She went to the sharpest men in her kingdom for help. Now it seems she will have to seek elsewhere."

"How do *you* know all of these things?"

"I have my ways," the woman said. There was something that looked like a sliver of starlight in her eye. It made Verity think her a little witch-like, after all. Of course, Olive would point out that the witches in fairy tales turned out to be good fairies just as often as not.

"If it were me," Verity resumed, "I would do anything in the world to help the queen."

"You're a little young to know what *anything* means, or you might not say so."

"Oh no! You don't understand. It would change my life. It would make everything better for my family and our shop, too. For that, I really would do anything."

"Then perhaps you should give it a go," said the woman with a sly lilt to her voice.

"Me?" Verity laughed, taking the suggestion for a joke. They were almost to the crossing, and she was a little disappointed that the curious discourse would have to come to an end.

But her companion wasn't smiling at her anymore. Instead, the woman looked very serious. It changed the shapes of the wrinkles in her face so she almost looked like a different person altogether. "Why not?"

"But I don't—I mean—it's preposterous! The very notion! What could *I* do?"

"You said you would do *anything*. Quite insisted on it! I wonder that you should shift your ground so quickly, child. I hope I've not misjudged you."

Verity suddenly felt that it would be a dreadful thing to disappoint this old woman. "I suppose," she faltered, "that I could try."

"Ah! Now you're talking sense. To try is everything. Failing is a good deal better than refusing to make an attempt. Don't you think so?"

"You remind me of my Nonna."

"That sounds like a compliment, young miss! I thank you."

They had reached the crossing. The old woman clasped Verity's hand in hers and squeezed.

"Farewell," she said. "And good luck!"

Verity retraced her steps, and it seemed to her that her path was lit up in new and wonderful ways. The same light was growing in her mind, and her step was quicker and more eager than it had been in a long time.

"Father," Verity said first thing when she arrived back home.

He looked up at her expectantly.

"Do you think that merchant has got rid of all his shoddy sole leather yet? I have an idea."

CHAPTER SIX

VERITY SAT AS tall as she could, wringing her hands in her lap. Nonna was on her right side, a silent but reassuring presence. Verity had never been inside the palace before. She wished she could feel more appreciative of her surroundings. But the long wait to meet with Queen Lucerne was taking its toll on her nerves, and the anteroom into which they'd been shown offered little in the way of distraction.

The room wasn't large, though two well-placed mirrors lent it an airier illusion. Plain wooden chairs were lined up against each of the four walls. Apart from these and one decorative framed map of the country, there were no other ornamentations or furnishings.

With not much else to look at, Verity studied the fellow supplicants seated around her. A pair of gray-haired men perched on chairs directly opposite, hands folded primly on their knees. To her left was a younger fellow with a tangled beard, who clung to a satchel as if he expected someone was going to try to snatch it from him at any moment. A girl not much older than Verity sat in the farthest corner. She wore a battered bonnet and did not once look up from her lap. A large woman in a frilly gown did not sit at all, but strode across the room in turns as if to better critique everything and everyone in it.

Verity wondered why each of them was petitioning the queen. She wondered how many of them would be granted their audience.

Will I?

She inhaled slowly, reminding herself what the peculiar old woman had told her and what Nonna had echoed. Even if the queen laughed at the offer Verity had prepared or did not agree to see her at all, there was no shame in having tried. She would have nothing to regret.

Verity strove to be patient, but each time the queen's attendant came through the set of double doors, her heart climbed into her throat, and each time he pronounced a name that was not her own, it plunged back down again. Several hours clawed by, and finally she and her grandmother were the only people who remained. When the attendant appeared this time, she half expected it would be to tell them to go home. *Queen Lucerne is an excessively busy woman*, she imagined him saying. *She has no time to see the likes of you*. Instead, he inclined his head toward her with an almost-smile.

"Miss Grandin?"

Verity stood up.

"Thank you for your patience. The queen requested to see you last so that there would be less constraint of time on your audience. Please come with me."

Verity's throat was very full of her heart now. The man's address made her feel important. She stole a parting glance at Nonna, who made a shooing motion, then followed after him. They went down a short hall, took a quick left, and the man opened a door. He stepped inside, and she heard him announcing her to the queen. She swallowed. Time had moved so slowly in the anteroom, like an hourglass with some obstruction impeding the flow of sand. Now that she was right outside the threshold of the queen's receiving chamber, it was as if someone had smashed the hourglass open, and time was spilling out too fast to catch.

The attendant beckoned Verity, and she stepped inside.

Queen Lucerne rose to meet her. The chair in which she'd been sitting was identical to those in the anteroom. She boasted no throne, no dais, no flank of armed guards. In fact, once the queen excused her servant, there was no one else in the room at all. The expression on her face, even her posture, suggested that nothing was more important to her at that moment than hearing a supplication from her shoemaker's daughter.

Though Verity's nerves settled, a sense of awe remained. This was the first time she'd ever seen the queen close up in person. A small portrait of her, attired with a sash and crown, hung in their shoe shop, but Verity thought her bearing more noble without the royal trappings. She curtsied low, and the queen returned a gracious nod.

"Miss Grandin," Lucerne said, sitting again. "It is a pleasure to make your acquaintance. Your father has served me well, and I admit that I am intrigued by your request for an interview."

Verity's heart fluttered. She was relieved to find that it had resumed its station in her chest. She had feared feeling foolish or insignificant in the queen's presence, but Lucerne's tone put all such fears to rest.

"Thank you for agreeing to see me, Your Grace."

"Of course. Now, tell me what it is I can do for you."

"As it happens, Your Grace, I have come in the hope that I can do something for *you*."

Lucerne's brows mounted into slightly higher arches above her eyes. She smiled. "Indeed! And what did you have in mind?"

Her good humor dissolved with Verity's next utterance.

"Your Grace, I understand that you are displeased with the number of shoes that we have had to make for you these many months. I am told that you employed the best detectives, and—"

"Where did you hear that?" the queen interrupted. Her tone was serious but not sharp.

"I gave an arm to a woman on the street last week. She told me."

"No detectives work for me, at present."

"Yes, Your Grace. The woman I spoke to said you'd sent them away."

Lucerne's brows were flattened low now, though Verity sensed her displeasure had more to do with the message than the messenger.

"Is this common knowledge in the town, Miss Grandin?"

"I don't think so. I've heard nothing about it, apart from what this one woman told me, and haven't repeated it to anyone else."

"What exactly is your motive in coming to me, Miss Grandin?"

Verity's confidence faltered, but she tried not to let it show. "I would like to be granted the opportunity to succeed where your detectives failed."

Up jumped the queen's dark brows again. She blinked a few times before answering. "I applaud your spirit in making such a request, but I cannot pretend to understand it. Has not your business prospered under my family's patronage?"

"The shop has prospered in one sense, Your Grace, but it has withered in another. My father and grandmother have to work so hard to keep up. Our old customers—our friends— have had to go elsewhere for their shoes. I know how it cuts Nonna and Father to send them away. We've grown so dreary, Your Grace. It is an honor to be of service to you, of course, but there is no joy in our shop anymore."

"In that case, it sounds as if you have every motivation to succeed. But how do you think you will fare differently from those who have gone before you?"

"Perhaps I shan't. But I'd like to try. Even if I don't succeed, none of us will be any worse off than we were before."

The queen fell silent, her head tilted in thought.

"How old are you, Miss Grandin?" she asked after a minute or so.

"Fifteen, Your Grace."

"And which school do you attend?"

"I had to withdraw from school last term because there was so much that needed done at the shop. They couldn't manage without me."

"Surely your family might have taken on another hand rather than resort to such a measure!"

"My father is very particular. Everything must be done a certain way, and he simply hasn't had time to train an apprentice."

"A girl your age ought to be in school."

"Yes, Your Grace. I'd rather go to school than work, much as I love our shop. My hope is to return in the next term or so. I want to graduate on time with my fellows, and go on to one of the colleges."

Lucerne looked impressed. "That is ambitious of you, Miss Grandin. Which school was it that you attended before?"

"We live in Donora Street, a short walk from the school there."

"In light of your aspirations, would it not be better for you to take accelerated courses in one of the city's private academies?"

"We count ourselves rich in many ways, Your Grace, but such a thing would be beyond our means, even if I were free to return to school."

"Should you like such an opportunity, though, Miss Grandin, if it were presented to you?"

Verity's heart thrummed. At the same time, her throat shrank. It kept her from any answer more elaborate than, "Oh, yes!"

Queen Lucerne folded her hands. "I confess, Miss Grandin, that I am inclined to think well of you. Your coming here with this proposal has shown me that you have initiative and tenacity. What's more, you seem to possess a deal of ambition. I will accept your offer, Miss Grandin, with one condition. In place of the pecuniary reward I'd have given your predecessors, if you succeed, you will receive a scholarship to Ridgewood. There is not a finer school in this region. After that, I can guarantee you entry to the college of your choosing. Would that be a fair payment for your services, do you think?"

Verity had given no thought to a reward. The restoration of her once-happy life was all she had anticipated receiving.

"Oh, Your Grace!" she squeaked, her hands clasped over her chest. "Thank you!"

"Do not thank me yet. Come back tomorrow, Miss Grandin, and I will arrange for you to meet with Sir Rufus. He will provide you with the parameters for your investigation and anything else you might require. For now, I dismiss you and wish you luck. I'm afraid you will need it."

Verity curtsied again, and floated out of the room. She smiled all the way home, and it never occurred to her that neither she nor the queen had once given direct reference to the six princes in the course of their meeting.

CHAPTER SEVEN

VERITY MET WITH Sir Rufus the next morning. He was far less gracious than the queen had been, and told her outright that he expected her to fail. She tried not to let this discourage her. Sir Rufus seemed to be the sort of man who would carry an umbrella with him on the finest day and anticipate a sunburn on the cloudiest. His were not words best taken to heart.

Verity learned that her investigation would begin on the first day of the next week. She would be allowed seven days to discover what the princes were up to. At the end of that time, she would report to the queen on her success—or failure, as Sir Rufus repeatedly added.

He made Verity sign a pile of documents swearing that she wouldn't disclose any confidential information to unauthorized third parties. He also provided her a copy of the princes' daily schedules, along with a diagram of the palace and a ring of keys that would give her access to the private living quarters of the royal sons.

"It's not proper," he'd huffed, as he handed the things over. "A girl *your* age going in and out of the rooms of boys *their* age."

But the queen's standards of decorum in this case were less rigid, and it didn't seem there was anything he could do about it. Dour though he may have been, Sir Rufus proved a fount of useful information, and Verity wasn't sorry to have met him.

She recounted the particulars of the interview to Nonna and her father, as permission to confide in them had been granted at her request. With the plan in place, and evidence of it to hold in her hands, she could hardly contain her excitement.

"I'm really doing it!" she exclaimed more than once to Nonna. Her father was quieter than usual, and she could not quite tell what he was thinking. She hoped he was proud, and that she would make him even more so. Though she wasn't usually much for daydreaming, Verity couldn't stop herself from imagining how happy her family would be when their lives returned to normal. In her high spirits, she did not envision anything other than a happy outcome to her forthcoming adventure.

On the day before she was to begin, Grandin & Son delivered a new shipment of shoes to the palace. Not until then did Verity's optimism waver. She bit her nails until her fingertips smarted, and when Olive baked a batch of custard tarts, she ate more than half of them by herself.

"Supposing my plan doesn't work, Nonna?" she fretted.

"Then I suppose you'll just have to give up," returned the wry Eleanor Twitchell Grandin, "and the entire world will perish in flames."

Nonna's wit soothed her nerves, but only for the moment. The day arrived clear and sunny, with songbirds for its herald. Verity could not share in their glee. She counted the idle, creeping hours until nightfall and tried to mentally rehearse her plans of action.

When she had asked Sir Rufus if she would be obliged to account for herself during the course of her investigation, he had told her she would not.

"You are granted free range of the premises while the week lasts," he'd said and then handed her an elegant brass seal with the royal insignia on it. "If anyone questions you, you may inform them that you are on the queen's business and show them this."

As she approached the palace for her first stint as a spy, Verity curled her fingers around the queen's seal in one pocket and her ring of keys in the other. Night had infiltrated the city. She would have preferred to conduct her investigation by the light of day, but however the princes were spoiling their shoes, they were doing it under the cover of darkness. If she wanted to catch them in the act, this was the only way.

Her father walked with her as far as the palace gates. "I wish you luck, Verity," he told her. "Though I know you shan't need it."

He said no more, and just like that, the shoemaker's daughter was on her own.

A man at the gate asked for identification before he let Verity pass, but no one else stopped her as she made her way toward a back entrance. Once inside, she took out the palace diagram Sir Rufus had provided. She'd practically memorized it already, but the feel of the wrinkled paper in her hand was reassuring. The royal family's private residence was located one floor up from ground level, in the east wing. Verity picked a route through lamplit halls until she found the appropriate stairway. A young sentinel was stationed there, but she supposed he must have been forewarned of her coming, for he winked and stepped aside, letting her pass without a word.

Either that, or he's a very naughty guard, Verity thought, as she ascended the stair.

Silence dominated the second level, and lamps were fewer. Verity noticed other differences, too. The furnishings and décor here did not look as costly or antique as in the main thoroughfares of the palace. The ceilings did not loom so far above her head, either. It was more like being in an ordinary home than a royal abode. Verity knew her history well enough to recognize that not every king or queen had practiced this kind of simple living. Lucerne was unique in that way, and Verity was prouder than ever to be both her subject and her spy.

She entered a practical-looking parlor and double-checked her map. She'd arrived, as suspected, in the quarters inhabited by Lucerne and her sons. A few flame-flushed embers still brightened the hearth, suggesting that the room had not long been vacated.

They must pass their free evenings here.

A piano took up most of one corner. Apart from that, a case of well-worn books, and a pair of ordinary couches, it contained next to nothing. Verity wandered around an equally uninteresting dining room and then what appeared to be a schoolroom. The latter housed three desk-like tables with two chairs at each, a globe, a blackboard on wheels, and plenty of textbooks. Verity lingered to inhale the chalky scent that floated on the air.

Just like my school...I hadn't realized how much I missed it.

Though she had permission to be sneaking about, the dark and quiet did not invite a sense of calm. Trying to ignore it, Verity once more unfolded her precious diagram and tiptoed down the hall that led to the princes' bedchambers. Another guard was stationed at the opening of the corridor, as still and expressionless as a pillar. He was older than the man at the foot of the stair had been and did not so much as blink at Verity when she passed him.

The queen's sons slept in two adjoining rooms. Verity approached the door belonging to the younger three. She heard nothing from within when she pressed her ear against the smooth wood panels. Peeping through the keyhole was equally unavailing. Nothing remained but to push her key into the designated slot. She flinched at the slight squeak it made in turning and the gentle clink of the shifting bolts.

She was relieved to discover that the door's hinges were well oiled and made not the slightest noise as she eased it open. Though she suspected the room would be empty, she still counted silence her ally. A clock ticked conspicuously through the dark while her pulse throbbed at double its pace. Parted drapes let in some moonlight from outside, but it revealed little.

Verity let her eyes adjust, gradually getting a feel for the room. She tiptoed farther inside, toward a shape that could only be a bed, and leaned her head over the shadow-blanketed frame. Her breath stuck in her throat. A boy-shaped lump reclined before her. For a full minute, she did not dare to budge. But as she saw the lump didn't move either, Verity swallowed her fear.

Why can't I see or hear him breathing?

She reached out and peeled back the coverlet. Instead of a prince beneath it, she found only a pair of misshapen pillows.

Verity did not like thinking that she had almost been fooled by one of the world's oldest tricks, but she exhaled loudly nonetheless. She arranged the covers as they had been before and continued to examine the room. First, she inspected the windows. This was mostly just to rule them out, for she felt certain that the princes were not making their escape by such obvious means.

When she peeked through the drapes, she found that the windows faced a spacious courtyard. It was bright with lamps and torches and populated by at least a dozen guards, one of whom was planted directly beneath the window. Remembering the cheeky young man who had winked at her, she wondered whether any of these guards might be complicit in the princes' escape. This idea she quickly dismissed. One or two of the queen's men might be capable of such disloyalty, but not an entire squad.

Verity left the curtains open for the extra light. Then she turned her sights to the floor, holding her breath and hoping against hope that her plan had worked. A decorative rug was rolled out over a large patch in the middle of the room, but the rest was all polished hardwood. Verity examined the area in front of the door with particular care. Her heart fell when she found no evidence there, but she did not despair yet.

As she worked her way around the perimeter of the room, she discovered what she sought. A few faint black marks appeared to the left of a dormant fireplace. The cheap sole leather had done its work. Looking up at the wall, Verity was startled to see a door there. It blended in with the wall so neatly that she had not noticed it before. From its position, she determined that it must open into the next room over. Trying the knob, she found it locked, and none of her keys opened it.

Puzzled, Verity slid the drapes back to their original position and left the first room to go investigate the second. She unlocked and opened the door with far less anxiety than she had felt the first time around. The arrangement of the chamber was identical to what the other had been, right down to the three beds rigged with pillows. She found evidence of more footmarks around the door connected to the first room. The space around the door to the hall remained unblemished.

If they are not here, Verity pondered, *and they did not leave by the door or the windows, then how did they?*

She stole back toward the parlor in search of a candle or lamp to aid her search. Now that she knew the princes weren't in their rooms, a light would be safe. An unwieldy glass oil-lamp had to be rejected, as did a heavy silver candelabra. But on one end table, she found a half-used taper candle in a copper holder. She lit it at the hearth and quickly returned to the eldest boys' room.

Holding out her light, Verity carefully looked over the bare floor, the carpet, the space under the beds, and even up at the ceiling. She spied a few shoe marks, but none seemed to point to how the boys were escaping, and nothing else was amiss.

The back of her neck prickled with perspiration.

There's an explanation. Why can't I see it?

Each bed had a bureau standing beside of it, and Verity advanced on the one nearest to her. Desperation made her bolder, and she began pulling out the drawers. She was startled to discover the first bureau all but empty. One drawer contained a few mismatched socks and a necktie, another a single book. The third held only some loose papers. Geometry homework, by the look of them.

Befuddled, Verity moved to examine the other two bureaus. Every drawer in each of them was full to the brim with neatly folded clothing and other common articles. *Too full*, Verity thought. Whichever brother laid claim to the empty bureau must have distributed his belongings between the other two. But why?

She returned to the first bureau, examining every inch with her light held close. She was on her hands and knees, peering beneath the piece of furniture, when she saw it. The front feet of the bureau rested on the carpet, but the rug ended about a foot away from the wall. On the hardwood floor, next to one of the back feet, was a distinct shoe mark. Looking closer, she found several more. Either the princes were going out of their way to stick their feet in strange places or the bureau had been moved.

Setting her candle to the side, Verity tugged at the set of drawers. It moved far more easily than she'd expected, sliding smoothly and quietly over the floor. Looking at the back feet again, she realized they'd been cushioned with felt. There wasn't a single scratch on the floor, but she spotted two more black streaks. Adhered to the back of the bureau was a leather strap.

Verity felt tingly with excitement. The pieces of the puzzle were scattered here before her. Now if she could only find how they fit together.

A bureau rigged for being moved in stealth…footmarks beneath it…look! There's even one on the baseboard.

She ran her hands over the smooth wood of the paneled wall. Suddenly, she heard a click, followed by a creak, and one of the panels popped open.

Verity started backward, knocking the back of her head against the bureau behind her.

Ouch.

Inching forward again on her knees, she examined the mysterious opening. It measured about three feet in height and two in width. She pushed on the panel to open it a little further, holding her candle inside. It vaguely illuminated a narrow, dusty room.

Sucking in her breath, Verity crawled in and stood up as far as her shaking knees allowed. The air reminded her of an attic: stuffy and warm. Holding out her candle, she found that the space was less a room than a passage, with only one direction to follow. Inhaling again, she went back to the secret door, reached through, and pulled the bureau back into place with the leather strap. Finally, she pushed the door until it clicked shut and hoped she wasn't trapping herself inside.

Verity held up her light and made her way cautiously along the passage. It brought her to a divergence sooner than she liked or expected. A new turning opened to her right, and another to her left. The path ahead continued only in the form of a hole in the floor. Verity crouched over it. A ladder led downward. Black marks streaked the top rung, telling her all she needed to know.

They would take the least savory direction, wouldn't they?

Verity hitched her skirt up by the hem and gripped her candle a little tighter.

"Don't fail me," she breathed, half at the fluttering flame and half at her laboring heart.

The ladder creaked under her weight as she inched her way down, down, down. Her courage, which had been dipping and swelling all night, surged again when her feet hit the bottom.

Oh! Another passage.

This one was a little larger than the first. The air put her more in mind of a cellar than an attic, though she didn't think she was below ground.

This passage was much longer than the first one had been, with more twists and turns than she could number. Verity had lost all sense of direction by the time it brought her to another opening. There she found not a ladder, but a real spiral stair made of stone. The steps were crumbling and uneven. What was more, they were wet, and so was the wall on which she put a hand to steady herself. She had to move slowly to avoid slipping or tripping, and she thought it took far too long to reach the bottom.

Yet another passage opened before her when she did, this the largest of them all.

It's quite as spacious as an ordinary hallway.

Cool drafts slid through, and Verity raised a cupped hand to protect her candle as the flame danced and quivered. The damp was worse at this level. Puddles lurked everywhere, some a good inch or so deep. As she continued forward, occasionally tripping or skidding, often kicking loose rocks and stubbing her toes on the uneven floor, she was no longer surprised at the princes' knack for ruining their shoes. Her own were wet through and taking a merciless scuffing.

Verity lost track of time and distance and everything as she trudged on.

This isn't just a passage, she decided. *It's a tunnel. An underground tunnel!*

She began to fear that she would never find the end of it or that there was some side passage she'd missed. A shadow swept around Verity from behind. Perhaps it had just been the dancing candlelight playing tricks on her eyes, but she couldn't be sure. She was hit with the inconvenient recollection of stories that Nonna used to tell her about giant creatures with bat wings and sharp fangs that hid in dark places waiting to ambush adventurers. She swallowed.

This is just the sort of place a grue would lurk. If they really existed…which they don't.

She shuddered and picked up her pace. Soothed by her own movement, Verity's thoughts returned to the princes. Bitterness crept through her like cold. Her muscles stiffened, and she clenched her teeth. To think that they were spending their nights running around such horrid dark places whilst their mother worried sick about them!

To that point, the tunnel had run in an almost straight line. Verity's thoughts took a tumble when she looked into the gloom ahead and saw a sharp turn. At the very same moment, an air current swept by her, extinguishing her candle. Verity's knees trembled.

She stepped forward into the dark, still holding out the useless candle as if it might make a difference somehow.

Is that light ahead? Or are my eyes just adjusting to the dark?

She went on, and the light became unmistakable. The open night was not a thing she considered as being bright, as it was most naturally held in comparison to the clarity of sun and day. But in contrast with the darkness of an underground tunnel, the light of night was a brilliant thing indeed. Verity gravitated toward it like a moth to a flame, until an opening yawned before her.

Another decrepit stair, illuminated by pale moonbeams, led up. She hesitated at its foot. The ringing of laughter tumbled down around her. And that was not all...a lively jig was playing! She could single out a pipe and a fiddle from between the voices. It was more noise than six people could make, even six naughty princes. Verity's curiosity wielded her like a marionette, and she moved up the steps. Sound and light both grew, reaching their peak at the top. Verity could see nothing at first, apart from a section of stone wall immediately in front of her. It tricked her, for a moment, into thinking she was indoors. But the moon above and spongy turf below told her otherwise.

Verity took several deep breaths, stepped around the crumbling wall that faced her...and stopped short.

CHAPTER EIGHT

V ERITY STOOD IN the midst of a ruin. Apart from a few walls, not much was left of the once-majestic structure. Some leftover patches of roof still arched here and there overhead, but she could see the moon and stars through them when she looked up. The floor hadn't fared much better. Though some of the original tile remained, it had mostly given way to a carpet of sod.

Tall cathedral windows—their glass long gone—and pillared arches hinted to Verity that the place had once been an abbey or chapel. Ivy encircled its columns, and lichen dappled its stones. A young ash tree grew in the place of one wall, its roots making free to invite themselves inside. Other shrubs and plants were already quite at home within the remaining facades of the ruin. In the middle of the main chamber was an open space, oblong in shape. The earth was worn smooth there, and Verity could see why.

Between twenty and thirty boys and girls, all around the same age as Verity, filled the hall, and most of them were dancing. The pipe and fiddle which Verity had heard were played by a boy and girl beneath one of the larger arches in the middle of the room. The dancers whirled about, faces flushed, mouths merry. They had all the light they needed in a terrific jumble of candles, torches, and lamps that hung from the walls, perched on windowsills, and wreathed the bases of columns. At one end of the room were the remnants of an altar that had been repurposed for a buffet counter, spread with hand pies, biscuits, buns, and apples.

Verity's head throbbed. She felt as if she'd stepped out of the real world and entered a land of fairies and enchantment. Shuffling to the nearest window, she tried to collect her senses. It offered her the prospect of a snug, night-blanketed meadow. The river gurgled just beyond sight, which told her that she must be east of the town. The main road and crossing could not be far. This knowledge, in combination with a few inhalations of fresh air, calmed her head. She turned back around to study the crowd.

None of the boys or girls wore clothing that was rich or fine, but their coats were smart and their dresses neat. Verity's own apparel made for a poor comparison at the moment. The dust on her deep-blue skirt was as conspicuous as a fly in pudding, and she tried in vain to sweep it clean. She wrapped her cardigan closer around her, hoping that the missing button in the front wasn't too obvious. She had dressed for stealth and comfort, not an elaborate clandestine soiree. The best she could do now was remain invisible. She pressed her back against the wall and observed the festivities from the shadows.

As she further scrutinized the faces, Verity was relieved to find none she recognized. She couldn't guess where any of the guests came from, but at least they were not of her school or neighborhood. Her only moment's panic came upon glimpsing a tall fellow with agreeable features that plucked a chord in her memories. He looked like a solicitor's son who had attended her school for a year or so. His name, if she remembered aright, was Archie, but he had been two grades ahead of her. Verity released a breath. If it *was* him, there was little chance he'd recognize her.

Two figures gamboling amongst the rest were decidedly shorter. They looked to be about ten and twelve years old, with identically tousled brown hair and laughing mouths.

They're not just brothers, Verity concluded. They're princes…the youngest two.

The boys showed no interest in the dancing, rather more so in the food, and at one point appeared to be having a contest to decide who could hold a handstand the longest. The smaller boy—*Prince Demetris*, Verity told herself—emerged dizzily victorious.

But where are the others?

It took a minute of careful searching, but at last she spotted the eldest three. Enough resemblance existed between the trio to confirm they were brothers, and they stood up straighter than most of the other boys in the room. Apart from that, and their trim haircuts, there was little to distinguish them. Their coats and trousers, though well made, were no finer than those a draper's son might wear. The real confirmation, of course, was their shoes. Verity could tell her father's handiwork anywhere.

Having singled them out, Verity's satisfaction quickly turned to horror as she realized that the boys had discovered her, too. They conversed in a huddle, casting curious looks in her direction. At first, she thought they were scoffing at her dingy clothes. Then a more obvious reason surfaced to rattle her composure. She was a stranger, after all, and this gathering a secret one. They were probably seconds away from confronting her. And what was she to say? How was she to explain her presence? Verity turned away from their scrutiny and pretended to admire her surroundings while deciding what to do.

I have nothing to fear from them, she reminded herself. *It is quite the other way around.*

Had Verity been privy to what the three princes were *actually* saying about her, it is hard to say what she would have thought.

"Who's that girl?" Christopher was first to say. "I've never seen her before."

"The ginger one?" asked Augustin.

Marcus clicked his tongue. "You know what they say about those."

"What?"

"Hot-tempered and sharp-tongued. Can't trust 'em farther than you can spit."

"That's nothing but a lousy stereotype," Christopher admonished him. "You can see just from looking at this girl she's a nice sort."

"Maybe. But she's more auburn, anyway."

"Who cares?" said Augustin. "She's pretty."

"Quite," Christopher agreed.

"I've always fancied gingers," admitted Marcus.

"Poor thing, hiding back there," resumed Christopher, standing on tiptoe in an attempt to improve his view of her. "She looks like she could use some cider and a dance."

Augustin elbowed him in the ribs. "Well, are you going to go talk to her? What are you waiting for?"

"Somebody's got to, Aug. But it doesn't have to be me. If either of you would rather—"

Marcus smirked. "Come off it, Christy. It's *always* you."

"I was only offering you the chance to step up, if you wanted to."

"Go on, already!" declared Augustin with a wave. "Everyone knows you're the host here, Christy."

"Heaven forbid I should take it for granted. You'd never let me hear the end of it!"

He departed his brothers' company, sweeping past the refreshment table before heading to give the pretty redheaded stranger a proper welcome.

CHAPTER NINE

VERITY CONTINUED TO feign interest in the crumbling architecture of the ruin around her. She crossed her arms, nervous fingertips tap-dancing in time with the pipe and fiddle. Had the princes lost interest in her yet? Or were they still watching? She tried to summon the courage to look over her shoulder and find out.

One of them appeared at her elbow before she could manage it, startling her into an undignified gasp.

"Hi," he said, smiling at her. The right corner of his mouth pulled back higher than the left so it looked like his smile was propping up the dimpled cheek on that side of his face. "You're a first-timer, aren't you?"

Verity's pulse drummed a staccato beat. She refused the prince's outstretched hand, opting instead for a stiff curtsy. "Y-yes," she said. "Your—Your Royal Highness."

He laughed. "None of that, please! We prefer to keep things informal here. My name's Christopher, but you can go ahead and call me Christy. Everyone else does. And you are...?"

Poor Verity opened her mouth, only to find her voice and brain equally paralyzed. She hadn't anticipated this. The princes may or may not have been too ignorant to know the name of the family who made their shoes, but she wanted to be on the safe side, and that meant using an alias. It meant telling a lie. Unaccustomed to deception of any kind, her mind tumbled in search of a name—any name. When she finally grasped one, it proved to be her mother's maiden name, and it was the best she could do to tack it on to her own.

"Bell," she blurted. "Verity Bell."

At least it was half true.

"*Verity Bell*. Well, if that's not the charmingest name I ever heard, I don't know what is. Suits you perfectly, too. May I call you Verity?" She bristled, and his smile turned into more of a smirk. "Miss Bell it is! Here, this is for you." He handed her a pewter cup that fit neatly into the hollow of her palm.

"What is it?"

"Poison."

Verity stared, and Christy grinned again. "It's apple cider, Miss Bell."

"Oh..."

Venturing a sip, she found the drink a delicious blend of sweet and tart that made her tongue tingle. She realized that she was much thirstier than she thought and took a deeper gulp.

"We do poison all our apple cider, of course."

"*What?*"

"Forgive me, Miss Bell. I can't help being a downright wretched tease sometimes. It's what comes of having five brothers. But I'll gladly quit teasing *you*. I just want to see you smile a little is all, Miss Bell. Not that a girl hasn't the right to frown if she feels like it. But this *is* a party. And you look so very ill at ease."

Verity forced a smile.

"Hmm," Christopher said, pinching his chin. "We'll have to work on it."

Her mouth settled back into a pucker, but the prince must have known better than to persist in calling attention to it.

"How did you find us?" he asked instead. "Who invited you?"

The dreaded question had been loosed. Verity cringed in its wake. She wanted to bolt, and only a concentrated effort of will kept her from it. "I—I don't really—" she faltered, with no idea of how to explain herself.

Christopher betrayed not the least bit of suspicion. He gestured in the direction of the dancers. "You must know some of the others."

Verity happened to catch a glimpse of the solicitor's son again. Her tongue pronounced his name before she gave it permission to do so. "Archie..." she said. "Archie—Graham?"

Christopher followed her line of sight, and she almost resorted to running, after all. Perhaps she'd mistaken the young man. But when he looked back at her, the prince was smiling.

"Old Archie, huh? I always thought he was a decent sort, but if you came with him, he's neglecting you something awful. That's not right."

"He didn't invite me," Verity said quickly. "I never—that is, nobody did. I just sort of—happened along. That's why I'm so—" She ran out of words, but gestured at her clothes and hoped he didn't question her haphazard explanation. She was in luck.

"Oh," he said, waving. "We don't care about that sort of thing here. I daresay you could show up in pajamas, and no one would bat an eye. We're all ragamuffins, in one sense or another."

"How did you ever—?"

"How'd this all come about?"

Verity nodded and avoided Christopher's eyes, which seemed so intent on holding hers.

"This used to be a secret place for my brothers and me. We'd come and just fool around, you know. Then one night the Kearnses found us. Do you know Nellie? And Pepper and Leona? No? Well, they happened along one night, and that's how it started. Pepper had her fiddle with her, and we started dancing. Next time they came back, they brought some friends. And now, we are as you see us."

She wanted to ask whether or not they were worried that someone would rat them out, but she lacked the courage. Instead, she took a different line of inquiry.

"Where does all this come from? The cider and every-thing, I mean."

"That'd be the fairies' doing, Miss Bell."

She wrinkled her nose. "You needn't keep poking fun at me. I want to know, really."

"The cider and the pies and such appear here every evening. I don't know where they come from. What's wrong with assuming that fairies leave them for us?"

"Only that there's no such thing as a fairy."

"How do you know?"

"Because they're made up. I'm sure you have never seen one, and I know I haven't."

"Have you ever looked?"

Verity grimaced. The sparkle in Christopher's eye was a perfect match for the winking dimple in his cheek. Olive, she thought, would get along with the prince famously.

"I assume," she countered, "your guests must be responsible for supplying the refreshments, if you're not."

"That is possible, Miss Bell. Hazen Shirley's father manages an orchard, and Joe Tinker's family are bakers. They might be my fairies."

"Don't you see them carrying it in and laying it out?"

"Never paid attention." Christopher shrugged. "I like to think it's the fairies that bring it."

Verity let Christopher take her empty cup and crossed her arms. She looked at the floor and wished that the prince would go find someone else to charm with his ridiculous fancies and catawampus grin. Alas, he seemed to have forgotten that she wasn't the only girl in the room.

"Do you dance, Miss Bell?"

Verity hesitated. There'd been but few opportunities in her young life for her to dance, but Nonna had taught her, and she'd always enjoyed practicing steps on the shop floor. Of course, she felt not the least inclination to dance right now. Not in this strange place, surrounded by people she didn't know. Not with her dirty clothes and damp feet. And especially not with one of the princes who had stolen her family's happiness. But she wasn't keen on lying about anything she didn't have to, either.

"If you want to know the truth," Christy said, misjudging her reluctance, "I never danced a step before I came here, and neither did my brothers. It was the Kearnses who taught us…" He paused and pointed to where Prince Marcus was leading a girl onto the dance floor. "Goose actually broke one of Leona's toes."

"Goose?"

"That's what we call my next youngest brother. It's a family joke, of sorts. Most of our guests still call him Marcus. To his face, anyway."

Christopher snickered, and Verity hoped that he'd given up his thoughts of dancing. But the next thing he did was set aside the cider cup and offer her his hand. The fiddle and pipe were warming into the notes of a new song. Verity bit her lip, daring to meet the prince's eyes. She was determined that she would not accept his invitation. Not for anything.

"Will you dance?" Christy asked, terribly mellow and gentlemanlike. He waited a beat before adding, "It'd quite make my day."

Verity didn't say yes, but she didn't say no, either. She wasn't sure how to refuse after he'd gone soft as pastry dough. Before she knew what was happening, her hand was in his and she was following him to the makeshift dance floor. Then the music picked up, and she was stumbling through steps, looking at her feet and trying to maintain as little physical contact as possible with her partner. Christopher, meanwhile, managed his end as comfortably and respectfully as if she'd been his sister. The rhythmic motions spun an ache into Verity's head. By the time the song was finished, she really felt dizzy.

"Are you all right?" the prince asked her, as everyone else dispersed and re-formed around them. She pulled her elbow from his supportive grip.

"Fine, thank you. I think I'll just sit the next one out."

"Of course. Are you hungry? There's pie."

"I'm fine."

Verity worked her way back to the shadowy edges of the ruin. She closed her eyes and pressed her fingertips to her temples. *This is madness*, she thought. *Dancing. And cider. And—and pie! The poor queen.*

She sighed and raised her eyelids again, disappointed to find Christy still at her side. She blinked at him and tried to reconcile his carefree impishness with the fact that his mother was a great ruler—regal, respected, and revered. Verity's heart was heavy. She'd already succeeded in doing what she set out to do, but could take no satisfaction from it, for she would have to return to Lucerne with the news that her sons were, in fact, rakish little devils. She had half a mind to call Prince Christopher out right there upon the instant, but her courage faltered.

To her relief, the prince was called away by one of his brothers.

"Got her to dance, huh?" Prince Marcus's voice carried as far as Verity's burning ears. "I'm glad I didn't put a bet on it." He started to say something about his brother's knack for wielding pixie magic over girls, but the remark found quick abbreviation in a shriek. "*Ow*! Ow, ow! Christy, cut it out. I was only—ow! All *right*! It was only a joke."

The snuffed candle Verity had taken from the palace parlor was on the floor of the ruin, right where she'd left it. She bent to retrieve it before edging her way around the crowd. Two other girls were making their exit, giggling and walking arm in arm out into the meadow. She followed them at a distance, through the long grass where a chorus of hidden crickets added their music to that of the pipe and fiddle. The girls disappeared into a grove of evergreens, but the brightness of their voices was as good as a lantern, and Verity continued after them. The music dimmed in her ears, further muffled by the huffs and puffs of her own breathing. Within a few minutes, she was out of the trees and clambering up a bank onto the city road.

She cast a long look back over her shoulder. The protective grove concealed the ruin from view entirely. Verity could only just pick out the festive sounds wafting through the still night air. With a shudder of mingled cold and disgust, she wrapped her arms around her shoulders and turned to make for home.

CHAPTER TEN

THOUGH HER FATHER had long since gone to bed, Verity found Nonna wide awake when she got home.

"You're back late, dear heart." Eleanor Twitchell Grandin smiled, pouring a cup of tea for each of them. "You must have found something."

Verity collapsed into a chair and inhaled her tea, scarcely drawing breath as she related her adventures.

"Oh, Nonna!" she said, when she'd finished. "It was just awful. You wouldn't believe the half of what I left out. They really are horrible boys. I can't think how I'm going to tell the queen about what they're doing."

"It sounded like an interesting place, though."

"I suppose it was. I didn't pay very close attention."

"It must be very old! And roomy, too."

"Roomy enough," Verity acknowledged, rubbing her chin. "It was rather like being outside and in a ballroom at the same time."

Nonna sat forward in her seat. "Pretty?"

"I wouldn't say *pretty*. But it had a sort of charm about it, I guess."

"And there were plenty of other young folks there, you say?"

"Yes, lots. It was shocking, Nonna."

"And music...with dancing?"

"Yes. All of that."

Eleanor Twitchell Grandin leaned back in her chair again and took a few long sips from her mug. "Did you dance?"

Verity grimaced. She would have preferred to leave that part of the story out. "Yes. But I didn't have much choice in the matter. You know how it is when a fellow latches onto you. And I could hardly refuse to dance with a prince."

"You had one of them for a partner, did you!"

"You needn't look so pleased, Nonna. I was never so miserable in my life. He went on and on the whole time, like there was nothing untoward about it at all. That's what bothered me most. None of them looked like they felt the least bit guilty."

Nonna took another draught of her tea. "What did he look like? Handsome?"

"Good grief, Nonna! You're as bad as any schoolgirl."

Eleanor Twitchell Grandin's mouth remained unmoved, but she couldn't keep the smile out of her eyes. "You're tired, my dear. Go on to bed. I suspect you'll have more to report after you go back tomorrow."

"Go back?" Verity cried. "But I can already tell the queen what she wants to know."

"Can you?"

"I know what those princes are doing. And I know how they're doing it."

"But do you know *why*?"

"It's because they're wild, undutiful sons."

"That might be reason enough for you, Verity, but I expect the queen would appreciate a little more insight."

"How am I supposed to find out *why* they do it? How do I even know there *is* a reason?"

"People have motives for everything they do. Doesn't the queen have a motive for trying to learn why her boys are ruining their shoes? Don't you have a motive for helping her? You can be sure, dear heart, that they have their reasons, just as you do."

Verity's shoulders drooped. She headed to bed, dragging her feet all the way.

Though she slept later than usual, the next day seemed to drag, too. Her imagination wouldn't quit ambushing her with all kinds of thoughts she wasn't interested in entertaining.

What if she did return? Would Prince Christopher accost her again? How could she avoid him, avoid *all* of them, and still figure out what their motivations were? What if they learned who she really was and what she was doing there?

The most serious question returned to her the most often. She even spoke it aloud to Nonna.

"Do I really have to go back?"

It wasn't really a question, though. The flash of mischievous wisdom in Nonna's eyes was the only reply Verity received. An unwelcome resignation made itself at home in her chest.

She knew what she had to do.

CHAPTER ELEVEN

DINNER WAS ALWAYS a quiet affair for the royal family. This particular dinner was more restrained than usual. Lucerne put all the accustomed questions before her sons. How had their studies gone that day? What had they learned? Had their free time passed agreeably? She felt like a performer confined to the pages of a second-rate script. She wished she could rip it to pieces and, instead, let loose the questions that so disturbed her. But it was no use. The boys were playing parts of their own, and Lucerne knew better than to hope any would break character.

Christopher was especially aloof. On most nights, he was the boldest of his brothers. Many a time, he even ventured to ask the queen questions of his own. How had *her* day been? Was anything noteworthy happening in the kingdom at large? Her answers rarely resulted in any deeper discussion. Conversation around the table was always sparse. But as she studied the distance in her second-born's downcast eyes, Lucerne found that she missed even his disinterested inquiries.

Slowly, bowls and plates were emptied. Alexander tapped his fingertips rhythmically on the tabletop, and the younger princes squirmed, exchanging impatient glances.

"You may be excused to the parlor," the queen told them, discerning their wishes.

The three youngest were up and gone in a flurry of squeaking chairs and hasty thanks. Marcus lingered a little longer, as if to exhibit his patience and maturity, before excusing himself after the others. This left Augustin and Christopher.

Lucerne attempted to speak of kingdom matters with her eldest, but his lack of interest was more marked than usual. His thoughts and attention were all directed toward his brother. The queen again took note of Christopher's faraway gaze, along with the quantity of uneaten food on his plate.

"Don't you feel well, Christopher?"

But he did not reply or even look in her direction.

Christy's mind was not on his mother, or his dinner, or any person or thing contained within the palace walls. He trailed a spoon in mindless circles through his bowl of soup. His thoughts circled in similar motions around a certain pretty ginger girl. Would he see her again tonight? Was she just shy of strangers, or was there some other reason behind her obvious uneasiness? How could he help?

"*Christopher?*"

The queen's heightened voice shattered his reveries. The spoon fell from his grasp with a clink. Augustin, who had gotten up from the table, gave him a wary look from the dining room doorway before escaping to the parlor. Christy realized with some surprise—and a pinch of dread—that he was alone with his mother.

"I asked whether you were feeling well," Lucerne repeated.

The prince gulped, comparing his own plate to the empty ones that littered the table. "I'm fine," he said. "Just a little distracted, that's all, Your Grace."

The way she studied him made Christy feel like a pair of spotlights were blazing directly into his innermost thoughts.

"And what is the nature of your distraction?"

Daring to meet those spotlights, he eased back into his seat. They weren't so blinding, after all. The queen was a discerning woman, but that didn't mean she could read his mind. For a fleeting moment, he wondered how she would react to the truth. He wondered whether there were other youths his age who actually told their mothers when they were thinking of a girl, and what such a bond must be like.

But the thought snuffed out as quickly as it had ignited, and the prince did what came naturally where his mother was concerned. He lied.

"I was thinking about the novel I've been reading, Your Grace. It's quite the suspense. A torture to have to put down, if you know what I mean. Only Mr. Hawk gave me all these pages of extra geometry problems to solve before tomorrow, and I know I won't have a spare moment for my book tonight."

"If you have schoolwork to finish, you had best go and do it. Your book will still be waiting for you tomorrow."

"Yes," said Christopher with mock melodrama. "I suppose I'll survive, somehow or other."

The queen flinched. She hesitated before admitting, "You sound so much like your father sometimes."

Christopher winced in turn. He never knew how to respond when she compared him to his father. He didn't know why she did it. Remarking on the resemblance clearly brought her as little pleasure as it did him. Pretending it hadn't happened, he rose from the table and wished his mother a good evening. Then he retired to the family parlor where the rest of his brothers had already congregated.

Cal and Tris were seated on the floor near the windows, engrossed in a game of jackstraws. Alexander was just as intent on playing scales at the piano. Marcus appeared to be doing schoolwork in a seat by the hearth, though Christy suspected his true attentions were elsewhere. Augustin had settled on the sofa with a novel.

As Christopher fetched his geometry and plopped down beside his eldest brother, he couldn't help wishing he had contrived some different excuse. Now he'd have to pretend to study all evening, just to validate his deception.

"What was that all about?" Augie asked in a barely audible whisper from behind the pages of his own reading.

"Nothing," Christy answered in the same tone. "Don't worry about it." Neither feared their mother joining them, but servants frequented these rooms, and guards were always lurking within hearing range.

The eldest prince lowered his book long enough to catch Alexander's eye at the piano. "Hey, Sandy, why don't you play us a fugue?"

Sandy reached for a sheaf of sheet music, quirking one brow. "D minor?" he asked.

Augustin nodded, then hid back behind his book as a series of forceful notes erupted from the piano. Christy had to lean in closer to hear his brother's whispers now, but this was a stunt they were all used to pulling.

"Something has sure been on your mind today," Augie said. "Or perhaps I should say *someone*."

Christopher flushed a little, then dared a grinning glance at his elder brother. "So what?"

"I suppose you especially liked her, then."

"She was a nice girl."

"And you trust her?"

"Yes."

"You trust too easily."

"And *you* worry too much. Why shouldn't I trust her?"

"No special reason. But it'll only take one person to ruin everything."

"I know, but Verity Bell isn't that person, Aug. She's not gonna run her mouth."

Augustin sniffed and turned a page of his book. It seemed he had nothing more to say on the subject, but Christy wasn't finished.

"Say, Aug? I think you ought to try your luck with her tonight. She didn't exactly take to me."

"If she didn't take to *you*, what makes you think I'll have better luck? Good grief, Christy. If you couldn't win the girl over, there's no hope for any of us. How do you know she'll show up tonight at all?"

"I don't," Christy admitted, a dull pain throbbing in his chest at the mere thought.

"Then it's as likely as not she won't come."

"But if she does, will you dance with her?"

"I don't know what you think it'll accomplish."

"She doesn't know anyone else, Aug. She's shy. Probably embarrassed. Surrounded by strangers."

Christopher made the appeal with full awareness of his brother's similar insecurities. The results were encouraging. A reddish hue spread as far as Augustin's ears, which were visible on either side of the book he still positioned like a shield over the rest of his face.

"She won't come back," Augustin said, as if trying to convince himself at the same time as his brother.

"But if she does?"

A ball of crumpled composition paper sailed toward the eldest prince from the other side of the room, hit his book, and landed in his lap. Down went the protective novel, revealing Augustin's visage in its full crimson glory. He glared at Goose, who was busily pretending not to be guilty in his chair by the hearth.

Christopher reached for the paper and smoothed it back into its original shape. The handwriting, complete with smears and errant drops of ink, definitely condemned Prince Marcus. But Christy ignored the culprit, instead handing the message to his eldest brother. It read:

ARE YOU TALKING ABOUT THE REDHEAD?

Augustin grimaced, crumpling the paper between his fists. Then he flung it back across the room, where it bounced off Marcus and ricocheted directly into the grateful embrace of a dwindling fire. Sandy began to plunk even harder at the piano keys, a sign that he was nearly to the end of the piece and for his brothers to wrap up their clandestine conversation.

"If she *does* come back?" Christopher repeated, his eyes wide and eager.

Augie sighed, with a roll of his eyes, which was as good as an agreement.

Christy grinned. "You won't regret it, Aug," he said. Then he opened his geometry textbook and began counting the minutes until they could once again slip through the secret tunnels and arrive in their own personal fairyland.

CHAPTER TWELVE

VERITY FROWNED INTO her open-doored wardrobe. She pulled out a lavender linen dress. It went well with her green floral sash and favorite light sweater. But it was wrinkled, and she didn't feel like pressing it. Back into the wardrobe it went. Out came a puckered-stripe cotton frock. Verity held it against herself, turning toward her looking glass. She never got around to wearing this dress as often as she wished. Perhaps this would be the perfect occasion?

"No," Verity sighed with disgust, flinging the dress to the floor. "Or I'll always associate it with this horrible ordeal!"

She wanted to wear something that made it look as though she weren't trying too hard. But choosing an outfit that gave the appearance of having been thrown together with no thought or effort required both immense thought *and* effort. Complicating her choice further, Verity wanted to avoid calling attention to herself.

"Why must you all look so conspicuous?" she complained to the clothes themselves.

None had come from a shop or a professional seamstress. Every last garment was the work of either her own hands or Nonna's. Verity was handy with a needle, but Nonna was an outright wizard. She believed in lots of pockets and odd buttons and fanciful collars. She believed in flounces, tucks, gathers, and anything that gave an outfit originality and dimension. Scarves were like a religion to her.

A lot of girls, the sorts who cared about popular fashion, whispered and snickered about Verity Grandin's clothes behind her back. But Verity loved the things she wore. Usually, she wouldn't have traded them for anything. Tonight was the first time she'd ever wished for a boring, ready-made outfit.

After an hour of deliberation, Verity finally settled for one of her better school dresses. It was a honey-colored linen, with a gathered neckline and off-center horn buttons down to the waist. Nonna had added a shaggy ruffle to the hem of the skirt and ribbon lace trim to the sleeves. Verity pulled on a cream knit sweater to guard against the advances of the evening air. Her hair, she braided and swept into a simple chignon at the back of her neck.

"My!" said Nonna when she appeared again. "Trying to make an impression, are we?"

Verity was crushed by the insinuation that all her efforts had been in vain. "I'm *trying* to blend in."

"Well, there's no reason to blush like that. You look lovely, my dear. With your pretty face and the brains you've got behind it, you could take on the whole world."

Verity thought it quite enough to be taking on six princes, but she hugged her grandmother and thanked her. Nonna had a way of looking at her virtues as if through a magnifying glass. Maybe she wasn't as pretty, smart, or capable as Nonna thought, but it did make her feel as though she *could* be.

"If you want to blend in," Nonna ventured to add, "you had better smile and talk to people and dance."

Verity frowned. Nonna's advice was harder to swallow than her compliments, even though they always seemed to go together. The magnifying glass had its drawbacks.

Outside, Verity threaded her way toward the city's edge, toward the country road that had brought her home the night before. There was, she reminded herself, at least one thing for which she could be grateful. She wouldn't have to creep through the palace and underground tunnels anymore, the same way that the princes did. It was a clear, cool evening, and she took her time walking. The cobblestone street devolved into one of dirt as houses and shops gave way to trees and hedgerows. Verity had never ventured very far out of the heart of the city before, or even beyond her own neighborhood. She'd never had any reason to.

As she gazed at the seemingly infinite night sky, thick with stars, she had to reconsider. *When this is all over,* she thought, *I'll have to come this way more often.*

It was with a sense of keen regret that she at last abandoned the road and wove through the trees. The winking lights of the ruin appeared ahead, beckoning her across the meadow.

Verity crept inside, keeping to the corners of the main room and trying to conceal her insecurity. Ten minutes crawled by in which no one seemed to notice her, and she breathed more easily. The previous night, she had surveyed her surroundings without really looking at them. Now she started to absorb a little more. The female guests—or perhaps the princes—had done an admirable job of sprucing the place up and making it look and feel like a real ballroom. Bouquets of fresh wildflowers stuck in old bottles were peppered between the candles and lamps on every flat surface. There was surprisingly little dust, and Verity didn't spot a single cobweb.

In one out-of-the-way nook, a boy sat alone with a candlestick, balancing a sketchbook on his knees and gripping a pencil in one hand. The music and chatter were apparently no match for his art. Verity watched him for some time, and he didn't look up once. Glimpsing his shoes and estimating his age, she realized that he must be Prince Alexander. His hair was fairer than that of his other brothers, but the royal nose and chin were unmistakable.

Verity couldn't help recalling the conversation she'd heard between the two girls in the baker's shop. Alexander was *nothing at all*, one of them had said. It was true that his appearance was not the most striking. Shyness veiled his eyes, and he had the blemished complexion one would expect of a fourteen-year-old boy. Despite this—or perhaps because of it—Verity decided that if she were likely to get along with any of the queen's sons, Alexander would be the one. He hadn't the look of a rebel or a mischief maker.

I won't speak to him, though, she promised herself. I won't speak to any of them, if I can help it. If I can just—

Her thoughts were sabotaged by someone clearing his throat behind her.

"Excuse me."

Verity turned around to behold the firstborn prince. He stood with his hands behind his back and his head and shoulders bowed toward her. Though he was tall, he had a frame that put Verity in mind of a boy with clothes he hadn't quite grown into. She remembered the baker-shop girl again. *Augustin looked as if he were on his way to a funeral*, she'd said. Verity could see why. The prince's eyes were a vivid shade of green, but devoid of sparkle. He didn't smile, and she couldn't picture what it might look like if he did.

Verity had to discontinue her observations, as Augustin was speaking to her.

"Christy told me that you're called Miss Bell."

She offered him a half-curtsy of acquiescence.

"I am pleased to make your acquaintance. I'm Augie."

Augie? Verity repressed a grimace. How she could possibly bring herself to refer to her future king as *Augie*?

"Would you do me the honor of joining the next dance with me, Miss Bell?"

She didn't feel like dancing now any more than she had the previous night. Augustin didn't look as if he relished the prospect much, either, and Verity couldn't imagine why he'd asked her. But Nonna's advice echoed in her memory. She supposed she could make it through one dance. What was the worst that could happen?

"Thank you—um—Augie. I'd be happy to."

They waited an awkward minute for the music to turn over, then Augustin offered her his arm and led her to the floor. At first, Verity hoped that the prince was not going to try to talk to her. He had nothing to say during the opening steps of the dance. As it progressed, however, he ventured to ask her a question or two. Had she enjoyed her first visit with them? Was the music to her taste? Did she have a favorite dance?

They were harmless enough inquiries, and Verity answered them without flinching. For a minute, she almost began to enjoy herself. The music, the dance, the flicker of candle flames mingled with moonlight...even the prince, courteous without being overly friendly, didn't seem so bad.

But it was only for a minute. The charms of Verity's surroundings dimmed as she remembered the queen and the shop bell. She remembered that the princes' behavior was shocking and abominable. Pursing her lips, Verity wished she'd invented an excuse not to dance with Augustin after all. As long as she was stuck with him another minute or two, though, she supposed she might as well make the most of it.

"Do you plan to throw a lot of parties when you're king someday?"

It sounded more like a demand than a question, and Augustin faltered at finding his demure partner in sudden high spirits. He mumbled an answer which she did not hear.

"I beg your pardon?"

"I don't think about being king."

"What, not at all?"

"Just not here. I have no choice but to think of it the rest of the time."

"Is it such an odious prospect?"

Augie abandoned eye contact with her. "No. Well— sometimes. Not odious. It's just—hard. To dwell on it too much, that is. Dancing helps. Usually."

"You prefer pleasure to duty," Verity said with the vigor of an attorney probing an accused criminal in court.

If Augustin had looked like he was on his way to a funeral before, now he looked as if he'd arrived.

"No, Miss Bell."

"You can't deny it's what you choose, though."

"Sometimes we need it."

He was missing steps now and nearly trod on Verity's toes. His hands had gone limp. His elbows drooped. He had a look that reminded Verity of the children she used to see bullied at school. Regret snuck into her heart.

"Forgive me, Augie," she said. "I'm not always this impertinent."

"Of course not," the prince answered, a little color returning to his cheeks. "Christy likes you, and he's never wrong about people."

As if by some strange magic, Verity happened to catch sight of Christopher at the instant his name was spoken. He saw her, too, and waved with a flash of his lopsided smile. She gritted her teeth, pretending not to have noticed.

Augie continued speaking, more animated than she had yet seen him. "Even just meeting him once, you must know what I mean. I'm lucky to have him. All of us are. None of *this* could happen without Christy."

"No," she muttered. "Even having met him once, I can't say that surprises me."

"It's just a pity I was born ahead of him."

"Why would you say that?"

"Oh, because, Miss Bell! Christy would make such a better king than I would."

The pipe and fiddle put the finishing touches on their melody, and the couples on the dance floor parted to applaud them.

"Well, I don't see why that should be," said Verity, raising her voice as they clapped with the rest. "In fact, I quite disagree."

Augustin tilted his head. "You do? Really?"

It was too late to think of what she was saying, and she assured him she thought he'd make a splendid king. Modest gratification flickered in his eyes. Before Verity knew what was happening, they were in place for a second dance. That was followed by a third, and the shoemaker's daughter felt as if she were partnered with an entirely different person. Augustin stood up straighter, moved his feet more neatly, and even smiled. His conversation improved, too. He pointed out others around the room whom he was certain Verity would want to meet, if she hadn't already.

There was Elisa Green, he said, an orphan and a sweet girl who was responsible for much of the decor. She had such a way with plants and flowers that they had taken to calling her Miss Green-Thumb. And over there was John Joseph Evers. He was a safe enough dance partner, but she mustn't let him show her one of his card or coin tricks under any circumstance. Of course, there were the endlessly talented Kearns girls, who were always the first to arrive and the last to leave. There was also William Keeler—a poor dancer, but a clever fellow with very good conversation, Cynthia Hodges—easily offended and prone to holding grudges, her brother Gilbert—invaluable in helping smooth offenses over with Cynthia, and their cousin Irene—who, though excessively shy, was fluent in three languages.

Verity was less interested in the people themselves than in Augie's knowledge about them. He had an uncanny ability for picking out the flaws and talents of others. Taking into consideration the fact that he was also intelligent, unaffected, and unflinchingly polite, Verity had to admit that he probably *would* turn into a good king one day. Yet whenever she tried to ask him about himself, he always turned his answer into an explanation about how one or another of his brothers was smarter, stronger, or more capable than he was.

They did not dance a fourth time, but removed instead to the perimeter of the room. The prince brought Verity a cup of cider, and they stood watching the other pairs kick and spin. Augie eventually waved his thumb in the direction of the refreshments.

"Miss Bell, would you care for—"

A "No, thank you" was on the tip of Verity's tongue, but then Augustin finished his sentence with, "—a raspberry tart?"

Verity had a weakness for tarts. She hummed, feigning indecision.

"I think there are apple fritters, too. And some sort of cake."

"Only if you're going over there anyway."

Augie disappeared and came back with one of everything for each of them. Verity did not turn down the offerings once they were in front of her. Her opinion of the eldest prince might have improved, but not enough for her to care whether or not he would think her a pig. Such a raspberry tart would have been worth risking the judgment of any boy for, anyway.

When Verity had swept the last of the crumbs from her skirt, two boys approached on the pretense of greeting the prince. They had scarcely done so before they were censuring him for his monopolization of the new girl. Verity colored. So did Augustin, but he introduced the boys to her as Bert and Joe Heywood. Each of them had shaggy flaxen hair, an aquiline nose, and large blue eyes. If they were not identical twins, they looked more alike than any set of brothers she had ever met. Bert—or Joe, she wasn't quite sure—asked her to dance and swept her away before she could decide whether she should accept or not. He talked to her all the while in a way that didn't really require answering, or even listening, so Verity was at leisure to occupy her mind as best pleased her.

Joe—or Bert...it really was impossible to tell—had his turn to dance with her next, but she still thought of Prince Augustin. She thought of him, in truth, as long as the evening lasted, even as she walked back toward the city.

In their quiet home above the shoe shop, Nonna was there to meet her again, with at least as many questions as before.

"It was so odd, Nonna," Verity mused. "Not what I expected at all. Augie isn't like the others."

"Augie?"

Fountains of heat sprang into Verity's cheeks. "They all have these silly nicknames. I meant Prince Augustin. But that's not the point."

"The point is that you liked him."

"No! I mean, yes. I *did*. But what I meant to say was that I feel sorry for him. I'm sure he just goes along with what his brothers like to do. It isn't his fault that they are so disagreeable."

"I thought you hadn't met the rest of them, yet."

"No. But it's not hard to see what they're all like." Verity, remembering the quiet Alexander, felt a twinge of doubt even as she spoke.

Nonna must have detected the hesitation, because she said, "You have five nights left before you have to report to the queen. And four princes left to meet."

"I don't *want* to meet them."

"You didn't want to meet this one, either."

Verity crossed her arms and bit her lips. "I didn't start this to make friends, Nonna."

"I only want you to do what's right, my dear. I want you to keep your eyes and ears open. Your heart, too. Not just now, but all your life. Don't be afraid to admit when you are wrong, either. It's the only way to ever learn anything."

Verity was doubtful. How much difference could keeping her heart and mind open possibly make? But she wasn't the sort of girl to chuck advice back in the faces of her elders. And Nonna sounded so certain. Verity could only sigh.

"I'll try, Nonna."

Five nights, four princes. Who would be next?

CHAPTER THIRTEEN

VERITY DIDN'T INTEND to ignore her grandmother's words of wisdom. But she wasn't about to give up her own ideas, either. She would get to know the rest of the princes, if only to prove that she was right about them. And if the queen desired more than just the superficial details of her boys' transgressions, then Verity might as well do her best to supply them.

The dancing and music were in full swing when she arrived at the ruin for the third night, but she was determined not to dance. Instead, she found a shadowy nook where she was not likely to be noticed. Alexander was occupied the same way he had been the previous evening, hunched over his sketchbook, making rapid movements with his pencil. She wondered what he was drawing, but not enough to go and find out. If she was going to prove a point about the brothers' reckless motives, quiet Alexander was not the prince to start with.

The three eldest princes were dancing. Verity tried to pick out the younger two from the crowd. Cassiel showed himself soon enough. He was standing amongst the Heywood brothers and some other boys, making wild gestures with his hands. They were all laughing. Verity rolled her eyes, then focused on finding Demetris. Just as she'd begun to suspect that he wasn't there, something strange floated across her line of sight.

Is that a paper glider?

It was. The glider sailed across half the length of the room until it struck a column, plunged to the floor, and collided with a candle.

Verity sucked in her breath, stole over to the scene of the minuscule disaster, and stamped out the now flaming glider. She turned to see where it might have come from, furrowing her brow. Someone had dropped it from above the heads of the rest of the crowd, but how?

"Oh, hey—" said a young voice from behind her. "My glider!"

Prince Demetris materialized at her feet, stooping to examine the crumpled, half-burnt remains of his creation.

"Where did *you* come from?" asked Verity.

He looked up at her with an irreverent glare and shrugged. "You ruined my glider," he said, straightening. "You stomped on it!"

"It was on fire," Verity countered. "I didn't ruin it. I put it out of its misery."

Demetris snorted. He looked like a younger version of his older brothers, with a few more freckles and a twitchier nose. His fair brown hair stuck out in all directions, as if he'd messed it up on purpose, and his shirt was untucked. His shoes, just days old, were already stained and scuffed.

"I was aiming to hit Sandy in the head, but there must have been a draft or something. It's rotten luck, too. She was a beaut." He sighed and flung aside the ruined glider. "Now I have to find something else to do."

"Where did you throw it from?"

"Hm? Oh, up there." He pointed to a crumbling ledge above two windows in one corner.

She gaped at him. "How did you—?"

"I'm good at climbing."

"You might have broken your neck! Did you ever think of that?"

The young prince betrayed no sign of concern or regret. Instead, he started digging through his pockets. Drawing out a small paper packet, he regarded it reverently.

"I wanted to save this for a special occasion," he said. "But I guess tonight will just have to count as one. Christy *does* always say you make your own specialness."

"What is it?" Verity inquired.

Demetris narrowed his eyes. "None of your business!"

But when Verity shrugged at him, as if she did not care anyway, he seemed to reconsider. Folding back one edge of the packet, he stuck his thumb and forefinger inside and brought them out with a pinch of brightly colored powder. Verity squinted at it.

"Looks like red pepper."

"Yep," he said. "The hottest kind. Gotta be careful. It was tricky to get hold of, and I don't wanna waste it."

"Oh?" returned Verity, certain that if she asked him right out what he meant, she would have no answer. She enjoyed the company of younger children, so this wasn't the first time she'd tangled with a ten-year-old. Demetris meandered casually to another obscure corner on the opposite side of the room, nearer to the refreshments. Verity followed him.

"Go back!" he hissed. "You'll spoil it!"

"How could I, when I don't even know what you're doing?"

"Because you're a *girl*. Girls don't care about jokes."

"I promise not to spoil your joke if you tell me what it is, Demetris."

"It's *Tris*," the prince said.

"Supposing you just tell me who the joke is on?"

Tris didn't have time to ignore her. He pulled farther back into the shadows and motioned wildly at Verity to follow suit.

"My victim has chosen himself," he said, grinning and pointing to where Christy had appeared a few yards off. He was chatting with his latest dance partner, a cup of cider in one hand. "*Promise* you won't spoil it?"

"Cross my heart," Verity answered. She was suddenly eager to learn what exactly the youngest prince had in mind. Tris put a finger to his lips, held up the packet of red pepper, then pointed back at Christy. She understood.

"Won't that make him very angry?" Verity cautioned in a whisper. Having grown up an only child, she did not know the ins and outs of brotherhood.

"Pff! No way. He'll think it's as funny as anything!"

Christopher and his friend wandered nearer, their conversation growing audible.

"It's a good turnout tonight," remarked the young lady. Verity recognized her as Cynthia Hodges, whom Augie had pointed out the night before. "I think I've seen a few new faces recently."

"I have, too," Christy returned. "Do you know Miss Bell? She's new."

"Who?"

Verity's heart turned a somersault. Why did he have to talk about *her*? If he didn't cut it out soon, everyone was going to know who she was. She made a frantic motion at Tris, who was ready to strike.

"Her name is Verity Bell. She's come the last two nights. I haven't seen her yet—"

Tris made his move unseen and then ducked back into the shadows. Verity clapped a hand over her mouth, and they waited in silence.

"—tonight," Christopher went on. "I hope she shows up."

"I never heard of her before." The young lady sniffed. "Where did she come from?"

"I'm not sure," Christy said, and took a satisfyingly deep swig from his cup. The next instant, his head jerked forward. Cider shot back out of his mouth in a million tiny droplets, most of which landed on the front of his companion's dress. Tears flooded his eyes and poured down his cheeks. He snatched Cynthia's cup from her hand and rinsed his mouth out with her cider while she looked on in horrified confusion.

Verity used one hand to smother her giggles, but Tris laughed uncontrollably. Christy whirled around, spotted his brother, and leapt to grab him. Tris wriggled free and scampered off. On the verge of chasing after him, Christy happened to catch sight of Verity. He looked back and forth between her and Tris, unable to decide which to give his attention to.

"Miss Bell," he half-choked, his eyes still overflowing. "There you are. How lovely to see you this evening."

His obligation to her thus fulfilled, he bowed and took off after his baby brother. Tris shrieked, and the chase was on. Verity watched as they careened around the room, occasionally running into innocent bystanders, but never letting it stop them.

"I'm gonna give you a licking like you've never had, Demetris Edgar!" Christy hollered.

Tris glanced over his shoulder long enough to shout back, "Only if you can catch me first!"

The other girls were none too amused, Cynthia in particular, but Verity couldn't help smiling. When both brothers disappeared from sight and she heard a slight yelp, she hurried in their direction. The pursuit had ended away from the crowd, where the ash tree grew in place of a wall. Tris was sitting on the ground, sniffing and blinking in an obvious attempt to ward off tears. Like any self-respecting ten-year-old, no doubt he considered himself far too old for crying. A bloodied knee showed through a tear in his trousers.

Instead of following through on his promised thrashing, Christy was bent over Tris, his brows knit. Verity would have been miffed with him, but she recognized that an equal share of the blame fell to her. She'd done nothing to discourage the young prince's mischief. She approached the boys guiltily, ready to offer what aid she could.

"What happened?"

"Tripped on a root," Christy explained. He was sitting next to his brother now, one arm draped around him.

"I'm *fine*," Tris protested, jerking his shoulders back. But he was still sniffing.

Prince Marcus appeared from out of nowhere to stand at Verity's side. "You're in for it now, kid!" He whistled.

"Button up, Goose," Christy muttered, pulling out a handkerchief and pressing it over the broken skin on Tris's knee.

"It ought to be cleaned properly," Verity said.

Tris whimpered at the suggestion.

"Rub some dirt on it," countered Marcus. "It's just a scrape. Your real problem is going to be explaining those trousers to the queen."

Verity was delighted to be able to scowl at Marcus, the prince every young lady seemed to fawn over. At that moment, she did not think him handsome in the least.

"Honesty is the best policy, *Goose*," she said, looking him straight in the eye.

He stared back, expressionless at first, before snorting and poking his youngest sibling. "You heard her, Tris. Better go home right away and turn yourself in. Been nice knowing you, kid. It really has."

Christopher looked between the three of them with a frown that was every bit as crooked as his smile, but he didn't say anything and Verity paid him no mind. She returned her attention to Tris, who had climbed to his feet.

"I could mend that tear for you as easy as anything," she told him, putting a hand on his shoulder, "only I haven't a needle and thread."

Tris perked up. "Maybe we could find them. Could you then?"

"I suppose."

"Fat lot of good it would do," Goose interrupted again. "The split would still show."

"Not hardly. My Nonna says I can work magic with a needle."

Christy climbed to his feet, smiling again. "I thought you didn't believe in magic, Miss Bell."

Verity gritted her teeth. "Never mind, then. Sort it out yourselves."

"We might be able to," retorted Marcus, "if you'd keep your freckled nose out of it."

The heat of her anger scorched any possible response to this. She turned her back and walked away, but not before she heard a final barb from Prince Marcus.

"Just like a redhead! What'd I tell you, Christy? They're all the same."

Verity wiped away the single hot tear that escaped her eye and ran for home.

CHAPTER FOURTEEN

VERITY HAD ALREADY spent more time with Prince Marcus than she ever cared to. But Nonna had talked her into devoting one evening to each prince, and she was not a believer in procrastination. If yesterday had belonged to Tris, then today might as well fall to the brother they called *Goose*. It would, in any event, provide an excellent opportunity for her to quit losing ground. The discovery that she actually liked Augie and Tris made her eager to shore up her defenses. No one was likelier to satisfy her preconceptions than Goose.

She set out earlier than she had the previous evenings, enjoying a leisurely walk through the streets of her neighborhood. Two figures loitered under a streetlight in front of Miss Dancer's Cheese Shop, but as Verity passed by, one of them abandoned the post and gravitated to her side. She cursed to herself.

"What're you doing, Grandin?" asked Erik Burns.

"Going for a walk."

"Where to?"

She held her chin up, walked faster, and made him no answer.

"Come on!" he said, jogging to keep up with her. "You can tell *me*."

"I could. But I do not wish to."

"Oh, you *do not wish to*," Erik echoed, raising his voice to a mocking, feminine pitch. "You got a date or something?"

"No."

"You want one?"

"*No*."

"You're so full of yourself! Just tell me."

"I've given you all the answer you're going to get, Erik."

"Fine, then. Be that way." He made a face and ducked down a side street.

Verity looked behind her a few times, afraid he would pop up again, but saw no sign of him. She picked up her pace, found the country road, and returned her thoughts to the third-born prince.

By the time she spotted Marcus after making her entrance at the dance, he was already looking at her. In fact, he and Christopher both were. They stood together, apart from the crowd, and the way they behaved made Verity suspect that they had been waiting for her. Their interactions looked, from a distance, something like this.

Christy: Mouth forming words, apparently along the lines of, "*There she is*."

Goose: Indifferent shrug.

Christy: Gentle shove, more inscrutable mouth movements.

Goose: Hand propped on hip. Right eyebrow cocked.

Christy: Not-so-gentle shove.

Goose: Both hands raised.

Christy: Crossed arms. Slight jerk of head.

Marcus abandoned his brother with no further gestures, approaching Verity abruptly.

"Good evening. I'm Marcus. You're Verity—sorry, you're *Miss Bell*. It's a pleasure to meet you, et cetera, et cetera." He paused, looking over his shoulder toward Christopher. "Do you care to dance?"

"I'd like nothing more," Verity replied in a way that clearly indicated the opposite was true.

The prince did not wait for a new set to start. He snatched Verity's hand and led her into the middle of the dance already in progress. She didn't flinch.

"Oh, by the way," Goose said. "My brother is worried you might think me ill-mannered after what happened with Tris last night. I'm sorry if you got the wrong impression."

Clever, Verity thought. He'd managed to apologize without having admitted to doing anything wrong. Her disdain masqueraded as a smile, and her voice oozed honeyed venom.

"Oh, no! I didn't get the wrong impression about you, Marcus. Not at all."

Accustomed to generous treatment from young ladies, he accepted this without question. Perhaps, Verity thought, he wasn't so clever after all.

After that, nothing more was said on that subject or on any other. His pseudo-peace offering dispensed, Marcus lost all apparent interest in his partner. He didn't even look at her. It was a wonder how he managed to keep up with the steps of the dance, the way his eyes were roving everywhere else.

Verity continued to smile, though her teeth were clenched. "Are you picking out your next partner?"

"Yeah," Marcus replied, after a distracted pause.

She stomped to a halt, freeing herself of his hold, and watched with satisfaction as he almost lost his feet. Not a few others saw what had happened, and some of the girls laughed and pointed.

The prince righted himself, looking at Verity as if she had cloven hooves and a forked tongue. A vein snaked visibly across the front of his forehead. "What was *that* for?"

Verity stepped out of the paths of the other dancers. Marcus followed close behind.

"You can dance with whoever you want now," she said. "Don't bother asking me again."

"Good grief, woman! What's your problem?"

"Maybe you should worry about your own problems. You're the one who just admitted you were eyeing other girls while you were dancing with *me*. Or didn't you hear the question I asked before you answered it?"

Marcus pressed a palm to his brow. "I wasn't paying attention."

"Then why did you answer?"

"Cause it would have been rude not to!"

"Of course," Verity snapped. "And you're such a proper gentleman. Excuse me."

She charged out of the ruin and into the meadow, not slowing down until she reached the first row of evergreens.

The third prince was everything she'd expected and more. *Goose*, she thought, squeezing her fingers into fists. *I'd give him a stronger name than that!*

The faint sound of snapping twigs and rustling branches stopped Verity cold. A dim figure appeared, coming toward her through the trees. But it tripped on a root and squawked out in a familiar voice.

Oh no. No, no, no!

Verity hastened into the grove toward the intruder. She had to cut him off, to keep him away from the sight of the ruin and the sound of the revels there.

"Erik Burns!" she said, coming upon him. "Did you *follow* me here?"

"Hello to you, too," he retorted, avoiding her question. "Do your father and grandmother know you're out after dark? In the middle of nowhere?"

Verity put her hands on her hips and circled around him so that he had to turn his back to the distant meadow to face her.

"Yes," she answered him. "Of course they do."

Erik seemed stymied. "Uh—well...What are you doing all the way out here? You were in such a hurry that I lost track of you on the blasted road. Gave up finding you and everything. Then I'm heading back, and I hear something in the woods. I nearly broke my neck coming in here to rescue you."

"If that isn't the daftest—ugh! I don't care to be rescued any more than I do to be stalked, Erik. Go home."

"Not until you explain."

"I don't have to explain anything to you. Just leave me *alone*."

Verity spoke in a heightened tone, hoping to camouflage any strains of music that might drift through the night. The same twig-snapping sound that had startled her before did so again, this time coming from the same direction she had. Prince Marcus appeared behind Erik. He stopped and looked from her to the interloper and back again. Though his face was lost in the shadows of the grove, Verity could tell that he was trying to size up the situation. Erik glared at the stranger, his mind similarly occupied.

"What's going on?" Marcus asked at last, looking at Verity.

Erik turned back toward her, too. "Who's *that?*"

Verity's mind raced, tripped, tumbled. Which was more important? To keep the truth from Erik or to keep it from the prince? Trying to sort it out made her head hurt. Finally, she turned to Goose, her cherished enemy only moments before.

"I—I, um..." she whimpered. "He followed me here." She couldn't believe how pathetic her own voice sounded.

Marcus stepped nearer to her but kept his eyes on Erik. "He's bothering you?"

"Well—um—" She sniffed with more mock emotion.

"C'mon, shop girl!" Burns exclaimed. "What's going on? Who is this guy?"

"I told you to go," Verity said. "You shouldn't be here."

He didn't budge. "Does your father know about *him?*"

Marcus took a step nearer yet to Erik Burns. He was a good head taller and looked pretty imposing in the shadows. "The lady asked you to leave," he said. "I suggest you respect her wishes."

Erik cowered. "But—but I—"

The prince took a final step in his direction. Cowed, Erik picked up his feet and disappeared through the trees. Verity exhaled in relief. When she looked back at the prince, she found his head bent toward hers.

"Are you all right?" he asked. The quality of his voice startled her. If she hadn't already known what a brash, conceited rogue he was, she would have sworn he was a sensitive, caring young man.

Verity started back toward the meadow. Though her face flamed, it seemed that disaster had been averted.

"I'm fine."

"Who was the creep?"

"Erik lives in my neighborhood. He's mostly harmless, but..."

"Not someone we want hanging around *here*?" Marcus finished for her.

She nodded. "He's all mouth."

"Well," said the prince, "something tells me he won't be bragging about *that* little confrontation."

"I expect you're right."

Marcus shook his head. "Boys like him are so pathetic. Bothering innocent girls and following them around, just because they need the attention. Desperate losers."

They stepped free of the tree line and back into the moonlit meadow.

Verity stopped. "How come *you* were out here?"

"Huh?"

"What were you doing coming into that grove? You were following me, too. Weren't you?"

The prince forced a laugh. "That's not the same. At all. I was just—uh—you know..."

117

"Following me."

"Well, you ran off so quick!" Goose exclaimed. "All angry and everything. I just wanted to smooth things over, you know. A few people I could name would never forgive me if I scared you off for keeps."

"I guess that's an acceptable excuse," Verity said. She started to walk again, but the prince stopped her.

"I know I didn't make a very good first impression on you."

"Or second. Or third. Or—"

"All right, all right!" He raised both hands in defeat. "I get it. You don't like me."

"You've made it pretty clear I'm not your favorite person either."

"Yeah." He sighed. "Well, you called me Goose. Last night, I mean. In front of Tris and Christy."

"Isn't that what they call you?"

"They're my brothers. They can get away with it. But coming from anyone else, especially a girl... I can't stand it."

Verity swallowed, averting her eyes. "I understand completely," she said. "I feel the same way when people make fun of my red hair."

"Oh." Marcus cleared his throat. "No wonder we get along so well."

A half smile stole over her lips. "I suppose there's no hope of changing that."

"Definitely not," he agreed, smiling with her. "My brothers seem to like you a great deal, so I have no choice but to take the opposite viewpoint."

"What? Why?"

Marcus sighed, rolling his eyes a little. "You don't have any brothers or sisters," he guessed. "Do you?"

Her mouth parted. "How did you—"

"I'm the third of six. Being right in the middle, you gotta be sharp. Got to be different, too. Find ways to stand out. I'd rather be friendly and agreeable around a girl like yourself. As it is, I'm forced to be rude and disagreeable."

"That's absurd," Verity said, unable to suppress a laugh.

"Wouldn't expect an only child to understand." He chuckled with her. "You don't have to find ways to distinguish yourself."

"Oh, please! You're plenty distinguished without the extra effort, Your Royal Highness."

She stopped herself short. What was she doing, bantering with Marcus like he was an old school chum? Just because he'd played the hero to Erik Burns's villain and shown a soft side and— Verity caught herself again.

Marcus was gazing at her, his expression identical to what Augie's had been when she told him he'd make a good king. "What do you mean? Distinguished how?"

She averted her eyes and hoped she wasn't blushing. "You *know*."

"Know what?"

"You're the prince all the girls whisper and giggle about."

"Oh," Goose said, his face falling a little. "*That*. Well, it's true. I can't deny that I drive ladies mad with my blinding good looks."

"At least you're modest about it," Verity countered.

Instead of parrying with another crack of his own, Marcus went on as if he hadn't heard her. "But it's only fun for so long. I mean—I don't mind what I look like. Sometimes I just wish…"

"What?"

"Never mind. Sorry. You don't really want to know."

"I do now."

At just that moment, Goose wasn't very goose-like at all. He looked like a young man accustomed to being overlooked one half of the time and looked at for the wrong reasons the other.

"Don't you ever worry that no one would really like you if you weren't pretty, Miss Bell?"

The words danced circles in Verity's mind, over and over, even after she was at home and in bed. She wasn't quite sure what her answer had been, only that she must have said *something*. The prince had gone on to tease her for being one of those girls who goes to all kinds of trouble to look good and then acts offended when a fellow notices.

By that time, she really was out of answers. Marcus had invited her back to join the others. But Verity felt as if she'd been punched in the gut, and the thought of dancing again made her feel queasy. He didn't protest when she told him she'd rather go home. On the contrary, he'd told her that he was sorry, for real this time, and looked forward to seeing her tomorrow.

Don't you ever worry that no one would really like you if you weren't pretty?

The insinuation floored her. Prince Marcus, the delight of Clementina and every other girl in the kingdom, thought she was pretty. It made it rather hard to hate him. At first, she scolded herself for being so vain, so easily flattered. But then, Marcus had not spoken the way *Eric* Burns did, with empty compliments. He had been sincere, vulnerable.

Verity started to wish she'd stayed a little longer. And she hated that, too.

It was all wrong. None of the princes were turning out how they were supposed to. Verity had to remind herself that *nothing* could excuse their deceitful rebellion. No matter what else the princes might be, no matter what motivated them to act as they did, they were ungrateful sons. But even as she thought it, discomfort squirmed around her stomach.

Even if it was a poor one, the princes had a reason for their nightly escapades. Would she ever be able to decipher what it was?

CHAPTER FIFTEEN

VERITY REMAINED GRAVE all the next day. Her purpose was as firm as ever. But not even the promise of a better future for her family could make her take pride in it anymore.

Eleanor Twitchell Grandin must have noticed her granddaughter's low spirits as she returned home from some errands that morning.

"I met a friend of yours outside the post office," she said, removing her shawl and hanging it on a peg.

Mischief brightened her eyes, and Verity could not but be distracted.

"Who, Nonna?"

"That squat boy from down the way. George Burns's son."

Verity groaned.

"He seemed very concerned about you, my dear," Nonna went on. "Wanted to know if I was aware of your going out at all hours. Asked if I knew about your meeting boys in the woods."

"What did you tell him?"

"I said you'd been meeting quite a few boys in the woods lately and asked him which one he meant."

"Nonna!" Verity cried, aghast.

"His face..." Nonna said, her smile graduating into a hearty laugh. "You ought to have seen it. It'd have done you good."

That was the first and last time Verity smiled that day. She spent the rest of her time trying to think of how she was going to uncover the princes' motives for rebellion. They trusted her for now, but if she wasn't careful, they were bound to get suspicious.

The evening did not get off to a promising start. Archie Graham was present again, and she'd hardly set foot inside before he was in front of her, reintroducing himself. He did remember her after all, and asked her to dance. Even though she hadn't known Archie well at school, she'd always taken him for a nice boy. That impression had come undone the first time she saw him partaking in the princes' clandestine gatherings. Now, her views had shifted again. Now she realized he fit right in.

Once released from Archie's company, Verity found herself accosted by both Heywood brothers at once. She was obliged to have a dance with each of them and then got stuck in a waltz with a burly fellow whom she'd heard someone else call *Boog*.

When she finally managed to squirm away from the dance floor, Verity's face was hot and her hair coming loose.

She was relieved to find an unobstructed path to the refreshment table, helping herself to a cup of ever-abundant cider. She hadn't planned on snacking, but raspberry tarts were part of the buffet again. She snuck one before backing into a corner to try to form a plan before the night slipped away from her entirely.

Prince Alexander, she noted, was tucked away in his usual nook. He'd traded his sketchpad for an old book but still had a pencil in one hand. As she watched him make scribbling motions over the pages, she thought he must have a bit of rebel in him after all. Writing in books was hardly an upright practice.

Before Verity could map a path across the room to tell him so, she found herself advanced upon instead. Not by a prince or another boy, either, but by a tall girl in a pale-green striped dress. A rosy circle glowed from each of her cheeks, and her black curls seemed to bounce less with every step she took nearer to Verity.

"Hi," the girl said hastily, sticking out her hand. "I'm Marcie Lyle. Really, my name is Marcenia, but I think my parents were horrid to saddle me with it, don't you? My parents own the repair shop on East Riverside. Pop fixes whatever comes through the door, and Mom does everything else."

Marcie paused to steal a glance over her shoulder. Cynthia Hodges and another young lady were watching them from a distance.

"Oh…well, it's nice to meet you," Verity said, trying to puzzle out the meaning behind this introduction. Marcie's overture might have looked friendly on the surface, but she didn't trust it. At least, she didn't trust Cynthia's narrow-eyed glower.

"You didn't know anyone else here before you started coming," Marcie stated. She said it like a student reciting in front of the class. It was a prepared line, without the least hint of a question in it.

"Actually," replied Verity, silently thanking heaven for Archie Graham, "I did."

This was an unexpected blow to Marcie. "You did?"

"Yes, I did."

"Well, who? And what brought you here? And where do you live? Who are your parents? How did you—"

Verity was spared from a further volley of inquisition as Marcie was cut short by a loud pop and flash behind her. She shrieked, whirling around to reveal Prince Cassiel.

"Oh!" Marcie cried, stomping her foot. "What on earth was that?"

"Just a snap dragon. Made it myself. I have more, wanna see?"

"I most certainly do not!"

Marcie stared the boy down. When he didn't back off or even blink, she retreated with an air of mingled failure and disgust.

"You're welcome," said Cassiel to the open-mouthed Verity.

"Thank you," she replied. "You're…"

"Prince Cal."

Verity looked him up and down. He grinned, showing off a snaggletooth in the front of his mouth like it was something of which he was proud. Cal's hair, like Tris's, looked like he'd just rolled out of bed. His sleeves were pushed up past his elbows, his shirt tails flapped amok, and his shoes had gone well past the first stages of disrepair. He was the only one of the brothers who had introduced himself as *Prince*.

"They're not *all* like that," he said, jerking his head in Marcie's and Cynthia's general direction. "None of the others mind your being here a bit."

"What a relief," Verity returned with a note of humor, though she really did feel relieved. She wanted to ask how Cal knew what the others thought of her, but he had changed the subject before she got the chance.

"Christy and them keep talking about you," he said, chewing his thumbnail. "Thought I'd see what the fuss was about."

"I'm flattered."

"How old are you, anyway?"

"I'm fifteen."

"Oh." Cal cracked his knuckles. "I'll be twelve in December."

For the common mortal, reaching the age of twelve was something that happened more or less on its own. Cassiel made it sound like a milestone achieved through superior skill and intellect. Detecting that the prince had a tendency to boast not uncommon in boys his age, Verity took quick advantage of the opportunity to test him.

"I've just been thinking how clever it is of you and your brothers to pull this all off," she told him. "Not just anyone could manage it."

Cal nodded in agreement. "We're not just anyone."

"How *do* you do it?"

"Christy. He's the brains. The heart of it all."

"Oh, of course. But what are you, then?"

Cal twisted his lips and looked at a patch of leftover ceiling as he considered, then held up both hands, wiggling his fingers.

"Ah! You're good with your hands. I should have guessed."

"Yeah. If I could, I'd train to be a magician. Or build machines. And I'd like to be a scientist, too, and make experiments."

"You've got some brains, too, then."

"If you only knew!"

Verity leaned in. "Knew *what*?"

Cal held his chin high. "You ever heard of Harold Chase?"

"The famous detective?"

"That's right. How 'bout Frederick Merkle?"

"He was responsible for finding that kidnapped baby last year. And busting that ring of diamond counterfeiters."

"Well, they couldn't bust *us*," the young prince bragged. "I outsmarted the both of 'em."

"You talk like they were the enemy or something," Verity ventured to say. "Why would a couple of detectives be after *you*?"

"There was another one, too," Cal went on, ignoring the question. "Aug said he used to be a spy. I forget his name. But he was old and fat. One swig of the special wine I left for him, and *zonk*."

"Zonk?"

"What do adults like wine for anyway?" Cal demanded. His attention did not stay in one place for long. "It tastes like medicine. Or poison. Or poisoned medicine. Anyway, the spy guy had it coming. Merkle and Chase, too. They learned their lesson. Don't mess with Prince Cal."

"You really *must've* been ingenious to take care of them like that."

Cassiel shrugged. "Miss Clement—that's my tutor— she thinks I'm an idiot, 'cause I fail her stupid tests half the time. She doesn't get it. There's more than one kind of smart."

Verity hardly approved of the way Cassiel directed his gifts. But she could not deny that *gifts* is what they were.

"You drugged those men? Is that it?"

He grinned in answer.

"How in the world...?"

"Wasn't hard. Like I said, old men love their wine. Uncle Rufus gave me all the sleeping tonics I needed. Not that he *knows* he gave them to me, but he'll never miss 'em. Tris helped me with sneaking it to their rooms. They never knew what hit 'em."

"How did you know they were after you in the first place?" Verity wondered. She knew she was pressing her luck. Cal was bound to suspect her if she kept it up. He was, as he'd been telling her all along, uncommonly clever. But as far as she'd come, surely her own abilities could match those of a not-quite twelve-year-old boy. She decided it was worth the risk.

"Our mother—" the prince said, then stopped short, as if thinking of what he was saying for the first time. Verity didn't allow him time to think of it too deeply.

"Do you know what this place is?" she asked. "Or what it used to be, I mean?"

Cal's shoulders relaxed. He smiled with half of his mouth, which made him look just like Christy. "I dunno exactly. Sandy said it was an abbey or something boring like that."

"You mean Alexander?"

"Right. He's the one who found it."

Verity glanced back across the room at Alexander. Had the quiet, inconspicuous one really started it all? She looked back to Cassiel. "He found it? All by himself?"

"Well, he found these papers in the library. That was the beginning."

"What kind of papers?"

"Mm—I forget the word. Like *plans*. From when they were building parts of the palace. They're super old. The queen doesn't even know about them. Sandy thinks one of our ancestors had the hidden passages put in 'cause he was scared of getting invaded and killed in his own bed. People were always trying to murder the king back then, Sandy says. Anyway, he got the papers out of the library and showed the rest of us."

"So that's what led you here."

"It's how we found the tunnel. Aug and Christy and Goose found this place after that. But it was *me* who figured out how to unlock the door between our rooms, so we could all be together." Cal's cheeks brightened as he related his own part in the events.

"Really?" asked Verity, no longer pretending anything. "How'd you do *that*?"

"I picked the lock with a jack straw and a pen knife. It wasn't that hard," he said. One of his brows quirked as he looked at Verity. "Anyway, I guess I get it now."

He answered the question in her eyes before it found a way to her tongue.

"I get why they all like you. You're different someway. Everyone else comes for the fun of it. But you're not just here to dance and all that. Why do you—"

"Cal!"

Verity was relieved to see Augustin striding deliberately toward them. She had a horrible presentiment that Cal had been about to turn the tables on her, and she mightn't have been able to dodge him. At Augie's approach, however, he forgot what he'd been saying.

Cassiel might have been eight years younger and two heads shorter, but he showed not the least deference to his eldest brother. Instead, he crossed his arms, looking up like a cheeky kitten might at a full-grown dog.

"Yeah, what?"

"What are you doing, keeping Miss Bell all to yourself? I've been trying to track her down half the night."

"It's not my fault if she prefers me to you."

Verity intervened. "Don't quarrel with Cal," she said to Augie. "I was all danced out, and he's just been keeping me company."

"*Yeah*," Cal said. "'Cause I'm a *gentleman*."

Augustin harrumphed and crossed his own arms. Apart from their height, they looked like mirror images of one another. "Well, you're the shortest one I ever saw."

Verity smiled and curtsied to Cassiel to show she didn't credit what Augie said. "Thank you for entertaining me, Cal."

Pleased, he bowed back. "Any time, Miss Bell."

She joined Augie in the next dance, then Goose for the one after that. Not until another with Archie Graham did Verity begin to think again.

What time is it?

It didn't feel late, but it must have been past midnight. Then she realized that she had not seen Christopher once all evening. She'd gotten used to his being obnoxiously near at hand, and it seemed strange he should make himself scarce all of a sudden. Scanning the room, she found him soon enough. He was sitting in an empty window frame with a cup of cider. Nellie Kearns bounded up to beg him to be her dance partner, but he refused her with a shrug and a smile.

Verity didn't realize how intently she was staring at him until he looked back at her. She flushed and shifted her gaze at once. Daring a single shy glance back, she perceived that he was just as embarrassed. The silliness of it all brought her back to herself, and she made a beeline for the meadow.

The open air cooled her cheeks as she navigated through the gently rustling grasses toward the trees. She was beginning to feel like the villain in her own story. It had never been her intent to befriend the queen's sons before she sold them out. Nothing was turning out the way she expected—the princes least of all. It was harder than ever to think of going back again the next night. But what choice did she have? No matter how her view of the princes might be changing, she still had a duty to fulfill.

Why did they lie to their mother? What lay behind their daring and dancing? She had to find out the whole truth.

CHAPTER SIXTEEN

"HEY, CHRISTY." MARCUS yawned as he bounced into bed. "Do you remember which chapters Mr. Hawk said we had to have read by tomorrow? Or, uh—which book the chapters were in?" He waited for an answer that didn't come. "I *know* you didn't fall asleep that quickly." Marcus propped himself up on his elbow and looked over at his brother. Christopher's eyes were open. He was staring at something on the ceiling that, though invisible, must have been very interesting. "Hey, Aug...I think we've lost him."

"Be quiet," Augustin grumbled, kneading a blister on the ball of his left foot. "I'm tired. And I don't care about your stupid books."

"You'll want to see this."

The eldest prince groaned but looked up. He snorted when he saw Christopher.

"Christy," Goose deadpanned, pointing toward the window, "the sky is falling."

"Great grues!" added Augustin. "It's raining blood out there."

"Aug, I think he's dead."

"Christy!"

"Chris-to-pher."

Augie put a hand over his mouth to stifle his laughter. Marcus didn't even try to disguise his.

"*What's* that, Goose?" Augustin said with a knowing look at his brother. "Miss Bell said *what*?"

Christy's head perked up from the pillow.

His brothers both chortled freely.

"Huh? What were you saying? What's funny?"

"Man alive, Christy. You're worse than Goose was over the parson's daughter."

The eldest prince had to duck as pillows hurtled at him from two different directions at once.

"Her name was Betsy, and I didn't care about her at all!" Goose snapped.

"Don't make fun of Miss Bell!" Christy said at the same time.

"We weren't making fun of Miss Bell," Marcus pointed out, happy to turn their attention—and his own—away from Betsy. "We were making fun of you."

Christopher fell silent, looking at the others as if to invite their further ridicule. It seemed he didn't mind, as long as they left Miss Bell alone.

Marcus couldn't really blame his brother. She was an exceptional girl. He lost his appetite for teasing.

Augustin said no more either. He simply flung the pillows back, and all three boys retreated beneath their covers.

To Christopher's relief, the subject of Verity Bell saw no immediate revival in the morning. Augie was even crankier than usual, and Marcus's eyelids looked like they were weighted, for all the trouble he had keeping them open. Though Christy hadn't danced the night before, he hadn't slept much either. Not that any of them slept as much as they ought, but Christy had been awake long after his brothers were snoring. He thought it excuse enough to hop on Goose from behind and travel piggyback to the breakfast table.

Christy had more than his usual trouble concentrating as their tutor, Mr. Hawk, drilled them in mathematics later that morning. Unfortunately, a man more suited to his name never walked the earth. He whacked his long pointer stick repeatedly on Christy's desktop, jarring him back into focus. When the lead of Marcus's pencil snapped, Mr. Hawk whipped out a replacement in no more time than it took to sneeze. He saw and heard everything. Christy was just thankful his watchfulness was restricted to their hours in the schoolroom.

Mr. Hawk kept one piercing eye upon him as he droned on with the lesson.

"You hire two seamstresses to sew a dress. One has experience and can complete the job in eight hours, but her apprentice will take ten hours. They work together for the first two hours, but then the experienced seamstress leaves her apprentice to finish on her own. How long will it take the apprentice to finish your dress?"

The boys started scratching out the numbers on paper, but Goose's pencil stilled after only a few seconds.

"What am I buying a dress for?" he asked, fighting back a yawn.

"That," returned Mr. Hawk, "is not relevant to the problem."

"Couldn't I be getting a pair of trousers or a new shirt instead?"

"If it will aid your problem solving, Your Highness, by all means buy a shirt instead of a dress."

Goose returned to his slate. Christy tried to focus on his, but he was laughing behind his fist. He thought he heard a snort from Sandy, too.

Marcus paused again. "But if I *was* buying a dress," he said, "I guess it could be a present for someone."

"A pretty girl?" Christopher suggested under his breath.

"Yeah! A present for a pretty girl. Not that I know any pretty girls, Mr. Hawk. I've never even *seen* one, myself. What about you?"

Mr. Hawk glared, leaned over Goose's slate, and tapped its surface with a talon-like forefinger. He had a passing scowl to spare for Christy, as well. "Why can't either of you show a fraction of the dedication to your studies that Prince Alexander does?"

The boys did not answer for fear their tutor would turn the question into an actual equation for them to solve. It wouldn't have been the first time. Mr. Hawk loved to extol Alexander's virtues in front of them. They couldn't resent Sandy for this, though, as he hated it even more than they did.

Sleepy as he was, Christy did not neglect to single out his younger brother as they were breaking for lunch that afternoon. Alexander was not a squeaky wheel like Goose or Cal or Tris. Even after years of studying his quiet looks, Christy could not always tell what they meant. He had developed a habit of checking in on Alexander's well-being as often as he could without being obnoxious.

"How'd you rest, Sandy-man?" he asked through a yawn.

"Better than you, apparently," Alexander replied. "Although Cal was talking in his sleep again."

Christopher draped his arm around Sandy. "Say anything interesting?"

"Not really. The baby pigeons were chasing him again."

"Ah, those relentless baby pigeons. You boys have all the fun over in that room."

"Based on what I heard through the wall last night, I rather think that isn't true."

Christy straightened and cleared his throat. "That was just—you know. Goose and Aug being Goose and Aug. As often as Augie tells the rest of us to keep our voices down after lights out, you'd think he'd know better."

Alexander shrugged. "I'm not going to make fun of you."

"That's why you're my favorite brother."

"However—"

"Oh, come on."

"*However*, I was watching you pretty closely last night, and—"

Christopher clapped a hand over Sandy's mouth. They'd shuffled into the dining room by now. The rest of their brothers were already at the table, and two maids were circling with bowls of chicken soup. Silence reigned until the maids made their exit. Even then, the conspirators spoke in hushed tones.

"That was a little too close for comfort, Sandy-man," Christy said, as if there had been no break whatsoever in their dialogue.

"I wasn't going to say anything incriminating. I'm not stupid."

"We know," Marcus piped in. "Mr. Hawk reminds us every day."

Augie leaned in. "What's this about?"

"Nothing," Christopher insisted.

"They were prob'ly talking about Miss *you-know-who*," Cal guessed.

"Yeah," added Tris. "She's everybody's favorite everything now."

The boys had all been taught not to slurp their food, but even their well-mannered sips sounded loud in the quiet that ensued. Christy's eyes met Augustin's, and they shared their mutual concerns through a series of arching brows and waggling heads. Goose's brows were raised for different reasons, and he turned to join in the smirks of Cal and Tris.

Alexander didn't look up from his soup. "I haven't even met her," he murmured.

"WHAT?" cried Tris and Cal together, so loudly that the three eldest princes shushed them in unison. Christy held up his hands, waiting until he had everyone's attention.

"They're right. I say that none of us is allowed to dance with"—here Christy's whisper disappeared altogether and he simply mouthed the name *Miss Bell*—"until Sandy's had a chance to meet her. All in agreement?"

Every hand went up except for Sandy's. And though he continued to gaze steadfastly at the bowl in front of him, spooning its contents into his mouth, his cheeks were pink as a confectioner's candies.

Alexander had no intention of presenting himself to Verity Bell in the way his brothers planned. Though curious to meet the girl, he was sure the introduction would happen in its own way and time. As was usually the case, he was right.

He perched in his usual spot at the ruin that night, a paper and pencil in his lap. Not long after the music had started, the hems of a lavender skirt swished within the range of his lowered gaze. A pair of well-made shoes peeped out from beneath. They stopped just short of him, but remained pointed in his direction. He could not remember the last time a girl here had approached him, and he guessed her identity before he looked up.

"Alexander?"

He rose to meet her. "I'm Sandy to everyone here. And you're Verity Bell."

She smiled in acknowledgment, and they sat down together. "I confess I've gotten awfully curious to see what you're working on over here every night. You must be quite an artist."

"Me?" he said, flushing. "No, not at all."

"You're just being modest. Can I see?"

Sandy shook his head a little but handed her the page he'd been working on. Her eyes widened as they scanned the complexity of intertwining bars, notes, and slurs.

"Music," murmured Verity. "You write music?"

"It's nothing exceptional."

She stared at the sheet for another moment before returning it to him. "How can you block out all the noise here? And you don't even have an instrument in front of you. That's extraordinary."

The prince only shrugged. Music came as naturally to him as breathing. He could never see anything extraordinary about his talent, as others seemed to.

Verity gestured across the room to the dancers and accompanying musicians. "Do you ever compose anything for them?"

"I tried once. A minuet. It wasn't popular."

He was grateful when she didn't pursue the subject further, as he had not much more to say about it. Despite—or perhaps because of—the fact that he preferred music to every other pursuit in the world, he found it difficult to talk about, even with his brothers. But they understood, and it felt as though Verity Bell did, too.

He noticed after a minute or so that she kept staring at his feet.

"May I ask you a question, Sandy?"

"Sure."

"How come your shoes are so worn out when all I ever see you do is sit here?"

"Goose and Cal go through theirs so quickly," Alexander admitted. "I usually end up swapping with one of them, since I'm close enough to both their sizes."

"You don't mind?"

"No, not at all."

"It's generous of you to share like that."

"It's nothing."

"Do they ever do anything nice for you in return?"

"We're brothers," Sandy said simply. It was explanation enough for him, but Miss Bell did not appear to understand. He tried again. "They would do anything for me, just like I'd do anything for them. They're all I have."

Verity still seemed dissatisfied. She kept swallowing, and an unsettled indentation marked the space between her brows. She spoke with a smile Sandy suspected to be phony. "You make me wish I had siblings. But you talk like you're all alone in the world. That's not true, surely."

"It's truer than not."

"What about all these people here? They're your friends, aren't they?"

"They're a good lot," Sandy agreed. "Speaking frankly, though, Miss Bell, all this could disappear at any moment. All of us know the jig'll be up if the wrong person were ever to find out about our little gatherings. We love coming here but it isn't safe to assume it will last. And it's hard to be true friends with anyone when you know you might lose them so easily."

Her eyes darted away from his. She wasn't comfortable with the present subject matter. Alexander wasn't either. He couldn't imagine why she kept dragging it out.

"What about your mother?" she asked, as if the question had an unpleasant taste and she wanted to spit it out as quickly as possible.

"The queen. What about her?"

"She must be there for you and your brothers."

Sandy sighed. "Oh, she's *there*. She's always there. But she's not *for us*."

He waited in dread of hearing what Miss Bell might say next. To his relief, she was silent, her gaze having moved toward the crowd. Following her line of sight, he realized that Christy was coming toward them.

"Ho, there, Sandy-man!" His brother grinned, placing himself on Alexander's other side. "Finally got to meet the famous Miss Bell, I see. I can't imagine what you're telling her to make her frown like that. You didn't bring that book of death poetry to read aloud, did you?"

"No," Sandy said. Though glad his brother had come, he couldn't pretend to be in the mood for humor. "We're just talking."

"About what? World hunger? Orphaned kittens?"

"Miss Bell doesn't—she doesn't understand us. Her parents are very different from ours, I think."

Christy's smile wilted.

"My mother died when I was born," Verity clarified. "It's just me and my father and grandmother. I think you're very fortunate to have a mother, that's all."

"We envy you in turn," Sandy said.

"What do you mean?"

"Sandy doesn't remember too well," Christy explained. "He was hardly five years old when our father died. But Da

142

was different from the queen. He was all hugs and smiles and games."

"I've never heard your father spoken of before. Not by anyone."

"Oh, no," Alexander said. "The queen wouldn't stand for it."

"That makes sense, I suppose. She must wish for his memory to be protected. To be cherished."

He shook his head. "Cherished? She wants his memory to be erased, more like. I'm sorry, Miss Bell. You look awfully shocked. But you must know that people don't always care for each other just because they happen to be married."

"Easy now, Sandy-man," his brother interjected. "You don't know what you're saying any more than Miss Bell does."

"Christy has a lot of cockeyed theories," whispered Sandy to Verity. "He believes in love and fairies...all that."

"Miss Bell already knows my thoughts on fairies," said Christopher, elbowing him playfully in the ribs before growing serious again. "I believe that the queen loved our father. But it was a dutiful sort of love. She had no genuine affection for him, any more than she does for us."

Verity squirmed. "How can you say something so unkind about your own mother?"

"I don't think it's unkind. It's just what's true."

"Well, I think it's awful of you. I'd be ashamed to talk of my own parents with such presumption."

"Hmm," Christy murmured. Sandy eyed him sideways. It was an unspoken rule between the princes that they would not discuss their mother in this place. But the rule was already broken. "I *am* being presumptuous, Miss Bell. Just not how you think. All my theories about the queen's feelings toward our Da are just that, see. She's told us more times than I can count that she never wanted to marry him. She talks as if she never loved him, either. I only suspect that she did."

Sandy shook his head, which was drooping considerably by now. "No one could believe it but you, Christy."

"I have no choice," his brother contested with a sober smile. "Not as often as the queen tells me I remind her of Da."

"That sounds like a compliment," Verity contested.

Sandy shuddered. "If you heard her say it, you wouldn't think so."

"Aw, Sandy," Christy said, bumping shoulders with him. "Good ol' Sandy gets it the least of any of us, Miss Bell. He's the only one who really has proper manners. You probably noticed that already. I've always figured Sandy was the queen's favorite."

"Augie is her favorite."

"He's the firstborn and the heir and all that. She has to favor him. But she loves you best."

Alexander had never detected the kind of favoritism from his mother that Christy seemed to see. She might scold him less, but that didn't mean she loved him more. She was the queen, not an ordinary mother. Whatever love she had for him and his brothers—if she had any at all—was kept neatly out of sight.

"That isn't saying much."

Doubt still lingered in Verity's eyes, but she looked as if she'd like to take Sandy into a motherly embrace herself. Christy opted for a less melodramatic course of action. He sidled up to his brother, hugged him like boys do, and mussed his hair.

"Well, Sandy-man, do I count for anything? You know *I* love you all right."

"I'm not sure you *do* count for anything, Christy," said Alexander, raising his head with an almost-smile. "You love everyone."

"Uh-oh. Miss Bell, you can see that he is beginning to show cheek. We try to squelch that sort of thing in Sandy, for fear he'll end up like Goose. Quick now, you must say something sincere and womanly to him."

Verity giggled and looked at Alexander, who had become bashful again.

"I like you very much, Sandy."

"That will do, Miss Bell. Thank you. Now, Sandy, are you going to sit here all night like a sad sack, or will you ask Miss Bell to dance?"

"Maybe she doesn't care to."

"Of course she does, stupid. Why else would she come? I'm sure she'd rather stand up with you than with me."

"But you *know* I'm a clumsy dancer."

"It's only because you don't do it often enough. Last chance, or Miss Bell will get bored and walk away."

Sandy cleared his throat. "Miss Bell, would you like to dance?"

"I'd be happy to, Sandy."

He didn't care for the dancing any more than he ever did, but Miss Bell made a pleasant partner. She did not try to talk any more about his family. Instead, she asked about which musical pieces and composers he liked best. She showed him a kindness that gave him an idea of what it might be like to have a sister. No wonder all his brothers liked her.

When their revels had concluded for the night and the princes were making their way home, Alexander brought up the rear. Christy lagged behind the still-boisterous younger boys to walk beside him.

"It looked as if you were having a good time of it with Miss Bell," he said. "Took me quite by surprise. You never dance."

"*You* talked me into it."

"Yes, but I didn't realize how powerful my gift of persuasion was."

"I suppose you thought I'd sit in the corner all evening and you'd get to dance with Miss Bell yourself."

Christy laughed. "I did!"

Sandy was taken aback by his sincerity. "Then why didn't you say something? I never would have—"

"Oh, never mind, Sandy-man! I got to see you happy. Miss Bell, too. That made me even happier than my original plan would have. Besides, there's always tomorrow night."

Sandy suddenly recalled a part of his conversation with Miss Bell from earlier that evening. The part where he'd told her that their fun could come to an end at a moment's notice. *Tomorrow night* might never come. The presentiment was unsettling, but he did not share it with Christy. Instead, he tried to forget about it and walked on toward home.

CHAPTER SEVENTEEN

DESPITE HER MOST fervent wishes to the contrary, the seventh day of Verity's mission had come. Tomorrow morning, she would have to report to the queen. She peeped through her bedroom curtains as usual before getting dressed for breakfast. Ashen clouds canopied the sky, keeping the warmth and light of the sun at bay. She checked again before lunch and yet again later that afternoon. The clouds prevailed. Verity could not have imagined any weather more appropriate for the occasion.

"It's your last night," Eleanor Twitchell Grandin noted as her granddaughter let the curtains fall back into place. "How are you feeling, dear heart?"

Verity's shoulders slumped as she made a noise that was half sigh, half groan.

"Is there anything I can do?"

"I don't know, Nonna."

"I might have a nice diversion for you, if you think you'd like one."

"All right," Verity agreed, though she maintained the air of a wilted flower that had been given human form and voice.

Nonna led the way to her own bedroom. There, she stooped over an old pine chest and rummaged inside. As far as Verity knew, it contained nothing besides a few spare quilts and old pillowcases. Could Nonna have something else hidden beneath them? Curiosity induced her to step closer and peer down into the trunk. Nonna displaced every last pillowcase, retrieved a package from the very bottom of the trunk, and laid it gently on the bed. Whatever it was must have been there a long time. It was wrapped in brown paper and a layer of linen. Some crumbling sprigs of lavender were tucked beneath a ribbon that was tied loosely around the package. Nonna pulled out the bow and unfolded the linen.

"It might not fit perfectly, Verity," she said, "but we can make adjustments."

She held up a gown of peach and ivory silk. Though old-fashioned, the style was of the kind that never stops being beautiful. It had a high waist and tea-length circle skirt, with a neckline designed to perch on the shoulders. The short, filmy sleeves had just the right amount of puff. Verity approached the dress on tiptoe, then let her fingertips brush across the delicate lace, the intricate embroidery and beadwork.

"Where did you get this, Nonna?"

"I married your grandfather in it and haven't put it on since. It's not the sort of thing most girls would wear for their weddings now, is it? Perfect for a dance, though." Nonna smoothed out a few wrinkles, then held it up to Verity and guided her to stand in front of a looking glass. "I'll give it a once-over with the iron. Then you can put it on, and we'll see how it fits."

Verity didn't protest. She changed into the dress and sat still while Nonna stuck pins in a few places. The fit was nearly perfect. Verity hadn't known it was possible to feel this pretty and this wretched all at once. She recalled one of her history lessons, about a neighboring kingdom whose peasantry had once overthrown their aristocratic rulers. Perhaps this was what it felt like to be a princess on her way to execution.

Verity remained mute as Nonna arranged her hair, then accessorized her with a tortoiseshell comb and a brass locket from her jewelry box. "A very old gift from my Henry," she said.

The final touch was a pair of lace gloves. Verity owned two pairs of gloves, but they were not like these. Hers were thick knit, finger-free, and of no determinable color. They were gloves made for warmth and industry. These were gloves of beauty and sophistication, made to protect ladies with pretty hands from the perspiring palms of their gentlemen partners.

By the time she was all finished, standing in front of the looking glass with Nonna beaming behind her, Verity felt beautiful as she never had before.

"I can't really wear this, though, Nonna," she protested, a blush banishing the paleness from her cheeks. "Not to that old ruin. It's just the princes and their ragtag batch of friends. Nothing fancy."

"You had better wear it! I've fitted you all up, and it becomes you perfectly."

"No one else will be dressed this fine."

"And what's wrong with being the loveliest girl at the party?"

"It will be uncomfortable. And I'll probably freeze."

"Nonsense! You'll manage."

Verity looked at her hands, blinking back tears. "Perhaps I won't go at all."

Nonna put an arm around her waist. "I'll wager a pretty dress isn't what makes you say that, dear heart."

A single tear made it past Verity's defenses and trespassed down her cheek. Her heart and mind were mired in thoughts of the princes she was bound to betray. She shook her head.

"This has been a trying experience for you, Verity. I know it has, and your father does, too. No one will force you to go, if that's what you decide."

"But?" murmured Verity, for she knew one was coming.

"You're my bravest, truest girl. I think you know that you must finish what you started." Nonna lifted her chin and smiled. "Besides that, we are Grandins. And Grandins do not do things by halves!"

"No." Verity forced a smile of her own. "We don't."

If Verity had felt conspicuous on her first night arriving at the ruin, she was doubly so now. Maybe triply so. All the other guests, boys and girls alike, stared at her. Some of them, mostly the boys, had their mouths open. Little Tris was the first to actually say something.

"Wow!" he exclaimed. "Look at Miss Bell!"

Verity's cheeks blazed. *No,* she wanted to say. *Look somewhere else...anywhere else.* It was novel to feel this pretty and flattering to be admired. But that didn't down-play the mortification of sticking out so much. Especially here. Especially tonight. She felt a sudden longing for magic to be real so that she might work an enchantment of invisibility.

Eventually the music resumed, the buzz of conversation filled the air, and the dancing picked up. Bert Heywood—she could tell him apart from Joe now—asked Verity if she could dance in that get-up. She said she thought so but would rather wait awhile. Bert translated this to mean that she preferred to wait until one or other of the princes asked her and went to find another partner.

Christy materialized beside her the next moment.

"Evening, Miss Bell," he greeted her. "You look—you look—"

"Ridiculous?"

"No, that's definitely not it."

"It's how I feel at the moment."

"You shouldn't. You're—you're the belle of the ball." He caught himself, and the corner of his mouth kicked back into the same lopsided smile that Verity had gotten used to. "No pun intended, of course, Miss Bell."

"Are you going to dance?" Verity asked, after an awkward pause.

His smile got bigger. "I am if you are."

She took his hand, and they joined the others on the floor. Verity's gown, far from impeding her, seemed made for dancing. The way the skirts swished encouraged her feet to move all the quicker. She felt as nimble as a fairy until the next song started. Her agility devolved back into awkwardness

151

as the notes of an unfamiliar folk number lilted from Pepper Kearns's fiddle.

"It's all right," Christopher said, reading her inexperience in the blink of an eye. He began to guide her through the steps before she had time to doubt herself. "Now cross arms like this...and circle around like that—you've got it!"

The pace was moderate, but Verity's pulse was drumming by the time the song had ended. Though the night was cool, she didn't feel it, not even when Christy let go of her hand and waist. He disappeared for a minute, only to return with cider for her. They drifted away from the activity of the dance floor, toward the ash tree. Verity had emptied her cup before she found the courage to speak what was on her mind. Her throat was still dry and grew tighter by the moment.

"Christy, why do you do all this?" she asked.

"All this?" he repeated, smiling playfully. Either he hadn't discerned the seriousness of her question or he was ignoring it on purpose.

"Why do you sneak away from home every night? Why do something so—so risky, just to dance and drink cider and chum around in this old ruin?"

"Because it's good fun, of course."

"But that isn't all. It can't be. I want to know—I want to know *truly*. Why?" She looked him full in the face, her eyes searching his.

As he met her gaze, his smile dimmed. He could neither mistake her sincerity nor evade her question now. Her heart pounded as she waited to discover what he would say or do, whether he would satisfy or suspect her. After the longest five seconds of Verity's life, Christopher sighed.

"Did you ever see a dog tied up or in a pen and think it wasn't right?"

"We used to have a neighbor who kept a great big dog on a chain in his courtyard."

"Did he ever get let off? To run free and play?"

"No...It was sad."

"*That's* why we do it, Miss Bell." Christy nodded.

"I don't understand what you mean," said Verity, her brow crinkling.

"Had you ever seen any of my brothers or me before you came here?"

"No."

"Did you know anything about us?"

Verity hesitated. "Nothing that was true."

"Exactly," chuckled Christy. "See, Miss Bell, we aren't given a lot of freedom. Or any freedom, in fact. Our lives are dictated for us. We're even locked in our rooms at night, if you can imagine. The queen—" His laughter was gone all at once, and he just shook his head.

"But she *is* your mother. And—and you don't even call her that. I've only ever heard you call her *the queen.*"

"I guess it does sound kind of heartless, doesn't it? Maybe if you met her, you'd understand."

I wouldn't, Verity thought. *I don't.* She struggled to keep the truth hidden from her expression. "Can you explain it to me?"

Christy drew shapes in the dirt with the toe of his shoe, hesitating to look at her straight. "I can try," he said at length. "But first I'd like to know what you're asking these kinds of questions for."

The lump in Verity's throat throbbed. His question was not steeped in suspicion or mistrust. He seemed simply to wonder about her motivations. She had known he would. She had tried to prepare, tried to invent a convincing lie. Now she would find out whether she had succeeded.

"Because I want to *know* you," she said. "All of you."

Once the words left her tongue, Verity was startled to realize that they had not been a lie at all. They were perfectly true.

Christy looked up, further surprising her with a smile. "That's fair enough," he said.

Knowing what she would be forced to do with his trust, she almost wished he had not given it to her. But there was no turning back now. Christy was already delivering his promised explanation.

"Things were more informal when our Da was still around," he told her. "I still remember him calling her *Luce*. But no one else has ever been able to get away with that kind of thing. Especially not us. She is the queen, and that's how she'll be treated."

"Can't you talk to her?"

"Sure. If she has the time and gives us permission. And we stand up straight and use proper grammar and don't say anything she'll disapprove."

"Oh."

"I wouldn't have you think that I don't—well, that I don't *love* my own mother. We all do. She's the only one we've got." Christy paused to swallow. The same painful conviction she'd seen in Alexander's eyes the night before lurked in his now. He loved his mother but did not know that she cared for him in return. "Things just are how they are," he went on.

"I don't know any other way to explain it, Miss Bell. We're like your neighbor's dog."

Verity tried to ignore the leaden ache in her chest. "Except you escape."

"Yes, we do. This is where we come to relax. *Breathe.* Forget all the schedules and the locked doors. My brothers need a chance to be themselves. Be free."

"What about you?"

"I just like to see them happy."

"And they're not happy, the rest of the time? Not ever?"

"We're not as pitiful as all that. We're fed and clothed and educated. That's more than some people can say. But..."

He couldn't find quite the right way to finish, but he didn't have to. Verity nodded. She understood now. Christy studied her.

"Are *you* happy, Miss Bell?"

She laughed in a weak attempt to keep from crying. "Why would you ask that?"

"Because," he replied gently. "I—*we* want to know you, too."

Thunder grumbled from somewhere. Though it sounded far off, Verity felt like its source was the depths of her own aching heart.

Your mother sent me, she wanted to confess. *Tomorrow I'll have to tell her everything, and you'll never come here again. And I'm sorry. I'm so sorry.*

She couldn't make herself say it out loud. At just that minute, she couldn't bear to think of Christy hating her. She did not hate him anymore, of course. It seemed so silly to think that she ever had. She'd put such energy into disapproving of the princes and the things they did that she'd never stopped to think that their side of the story might be worth hearing, too. She had thought of them only as rascals and rebels. She hadn't considered that their struggles and desires might be every bit as complex and just as her own.

One by one she'd gotten glimpses of who they really were, and all of her preconceived notions melted like snow in spring. She could not imagine why Christopher had been the last, why it had taken her so long to see his heart. She recognized now that he was the warmest of them all. Caring for him, caring for all of them, was not something Verity had prepared herself for. It brought a pain that she could feel not just in her heart or mind but in her arms and legs, her fingers and toes.

"You'd like to be left alone for a spell," Christy guessed, breaking a prolonged silence.

"Oh, no! I mean—I'm sorry. It's just—"

"Don't worry, Miss Bell," he said, already walking away. "I know that look. Sandy gets the same one. And if you change your mind, you know where to find me."

The truth was, Verity *didn't* want to be alone. It would leave her to her thoughts. It would hurt too much. She was secretly relieved when Marcus found her a minute later, begging to be granted a turn with the prettiest girl in the room. She accepted him without hesitation, letting the music and movement and laughter on the dance floor chase her guilt away.

That night, she danced as she had never done before. Two turns with Goose, two with Augie, one with Archie Graham, two more with boys whose names she did not even know. She danced until Pepper Kearns put down her fiddle and the piper his pipe.

The rumbling from the distant skies had already prompted more than half the assembly to take an early leave, but Verity could not bring herself to follow them. Those who remained stood about, ignoring the thunder, talking and laughing.

"It's going to rain," Verity heard Augustin say.

"Maybe it won't," countered an optimistic, freckled youth.

But not a minute later, the downpour began. Some rain-storms start out gently, building strength until they reach the height of their fury. This was not one of them. Verity felt no warning sprinkles. One moment, the clouds kept their own company, and the next they pelted the world below them with unrestrained glee.

Verity hastened to find shelter beneath the nearest stretch of roof. Nellie Kearns waved at her from a dry corner where she and her sisters fit together neatly.

"We have room for one more!" She grinned, squashing against Leona.

Verity shook her head. Nellie's friendliness and good humor scraped an even deeper pit into her stomach. She realized that the princes weren't the only ones she was betraying. She tried to lodge herself safely apart from the sisters, but there wasn't enough cover to protect her entirely. Dark wet spots multiplied on her skirts, and she felt the cold, sharp splats hitting her arms and face.

Then, seemingly from out of nowhere, the raindrops were thwarted. Verity glanced to her right. Christopher stood there, using his jacket like an umbrella to shield her from the storm. He said nothing, and his eyes were on the meadow.

From the expression on his face, Verity could tell that watching storms gave him the kind of pleasure that words cannot communicate. His own dampness was of little concern. As she blinked at him, she realized how close they were, how his arms were all but encircling her. Somehow it was different from dancing, and her face grew warm enough to make her glad that he wasn't looking at it.

The downpour soon tapered off, being the sort that spends itself in one great burst of passion. Christy lowered his jacket from Verity's head and draped it gingerly over her shoulders.

"Sorry," he said, plunging his hands into his trouser pockets. "I don't think it helped much."

"It did," she was quick to assure him. "Thank you."

She detached herself from the warmth of the jacket and tried to hand it back to him.

"You'd better keep it, Miss Bell. I don't want you to catch a chill walking home."

"Oh, no! I couldn't. Besides, you'll need it more than I do, going up those drafty passages."

He met her eyes suddenly. "You know about the passages?"

Verity's stomach lurched. "I—um—Cal told me about them. I hope you're not upset."

"No. I wouldn't have just anyone knowing all our secrets! But I'm sure I can trust you, Miss Bell."

"I—I should be going now, before another storm comes."

She tried to return the jacket again, but Christy shook his head.

"You take it, like I said. I'll feel better. I wish I could see you home myself, but..." He trailed off wistfully before clearing his throat. "You can return it tomorrow. And we can talk some more, maybe. If you'd like."

Verity was too miserable to argue further. She murmured her thanks and darted off into the night. Though she did not look back, she could feel Christy watching her. Warm tears glided down her cheeks, growing cold at her chin before dropping onto his jacket, which she clutched close around her.

When she reached home, her face was still wet. She went straight to her room, flung herself upon her bed, and buried her eyes in the folds of Christy's jacket until her tears ran dry and she fell asleep.

CHAPTER EIGHTEEN

THE SUN HAD cast away its cloudy mantle by the next morning, but its warmth did not touch Verity's spirit. No one in her household needed to ask what the matter was. Her father and Nonna already knew her grief. Even Olive, though oblivious to the circumstances, was perceptive enough to hold her tongue.

Nonna doled out comfort in hugs instead of words, and Verity's father did his best to support her with several solemn smiles. They walked with her as far as the palace, but she insisted on continuing inside alone. Her meeting with the queen was scheduled for noon. There was no wait this time. She was shown directly to Queen Lucerne's private study. Verity trembled through a curtsy and declined the chair that was offered her.

"What do you have for me, Miss Grandin?" the queen asked. Her voice was like the wind, not the less powerful for its present gentleness.

Verity couldn't tell if she spoke in general terms or in reference to the parcels she was clutching in her arms. Not knowing how else to proceed, she handed over the candlestick, keys, and queen's seal, along with a package wrapped in brown paper.

"This is a curious beginning, Miss Grandin," said Lucerne as she accepted them. "Dare I ask its meaning?"

Verity breathed heavily. "I am returning the things you gave me. And a candle I borrowed from your parlor. And—and Christy's jacket, Your Grace."

On her mention of the last item, the queen's eyes widened. Verity did not wait to be asked for an explanation.

"It rained last night, Your Grace," she said, forcing herself to sound composed. "Prince Christopher lent me his jacket. He would not take it back, and so I promised to return it later. There it is, as you see. It's been pressed. He—he expected me to give it back this evening. I thought it would be best to bring it to you."

The queen unwrapped the paper, letting it drift to the floor. She held the garment in her hands, looking at it with disbelief.

"May I take from this narrative, Miss Grandin," she said after a moment, "that your efforts have proven fruitful?"

"I can tell you all you want to know, Your Grace."

Every word that passed between them added to the weight in Verity's heart, while Lucerne's burden appeared to be growing lighter. The queen sighed, already relieved, and held her son's jacket close to her in folded arms.

"Go on then, Miss Grandin, if you please."

"I'll tell you what I learned," Verity said, "but it does not please me, Your Grace."

"What do you mean?"

"Your sons were not what I expected at all, Your Grace. They—they were good to me and—and now I must betray them."

Queen Lucerne lowered herself slowly into a chair, motioning her guest toward a seat opposite. "Perhaps, Miss Grandin, you had better start at the beginning."

Verity nodded. Swallowing and blinking, she then confessed all. She started by telling of the compromised sole leather that her father had used for the latest pairs of the boys' shoes. She told how it led to her discovery of the secret panel and then the passageway and the hidden ruin. This bridged into a description of the music, and the dancing, and the guests. She explained about the spoiled shoes. She even mentioned the cider.

Lucerne listened without interruption. Once Verity had finished, a long minute passed before she received any reply.

"Well, Miss Grandin," the queen said at last, "you have been most thorough. The reward we agreed upon is yours, and I give it with many thanks. You have much to be proud of."

"I don't think I have, Your Grace," Verity returned, the first tear trickling down her flushed cheek. "I thank you. But I cannot accept the reward. Not in good conscience."

"I understand if you feel conflicted, Miss Grandin. But this is no cause for such an extreme refusal, surely. You have shown great loyalty to me and deserve all the gratitude that I can give."

Verity could not help looking, for a moment, at the jacket that Lucerne still clutched. She took out a handkerchief to mop her eyes. Blubbering in front of a monarch was a terrible humiliation. But she couldn't help it.

"Do I have your permission to speak freely, Your Grace?"

"You do not need my permission to do that, Miss Grandin. I would have all my people be at their ease with me and say what they would."

"Then may I ask whether you grant the same liberty to your sons?"

Lucerne's head jerked back as if she'd been struck by an invisible hand. "They're my children," she asserted, "not my subjects. It is different."

"Yes." Verity nodded. "It *ought* to be different. But—but in another way."

"You speak with incredible presumption, Miss Grandin. I might remind you that you have known my boys no more than a week."

"That is true, and it grieves me, Your Grace, because I think I'm better acquainted with them than you are." Verity half-sobbed. "They feel smothered and neglected at the same time. Did you know that? That's why they escape at night. They love you. I think they would like to please you, too, if they thought it was possible. If they thought you—oh, Your Grace! Your own children don't know you love them. They're wrong...they *must* be. You're their own mother."

The queen was speechless. Verity's tongue flew faster yet.

"They would flourish, Your Grace, if only they had the room to grow. Do you know how clever they are, all of them? Alexander might well be a genius. And Cal, too, for that matter. Tris...well, Tris is every bit the monkey. Is he ever allowed to be a little boy, Your Grace? And Augustin… He is capable of so much more than he thinks. He only needs a little encouragement, Your Grace. Marcus just wants to be *seen*, I think. To be taken seriously sometimes. There is more to him than what shows on the outside. And—and Christopher...do you know how selfless he is? Or what a generous heart he has? You have six *wonderful* sons, Your Grace. They kept all this from you, but it was only out of want for a little freedom. That's all they're guilty of. I am far more guilty than any of them... They—they were so kind to me, and I was double-crossing them all the while."

Spent by her outburst, Verity sank back into her chair, sniffling.

The queen was not quick to answer. She gazed intently at Christy's jacket and clung to it more tightly than ever. Verity could see the creases around her eyes. When she spoke at last, her voice was low.

"I can't begin to set forth the difficulties of being a queen, a wife, and a mother all at once, Miss Grandin. I had not much choice in becoming any of the three, yet I have always tried to do what was right in each of the roles thrust upon me. I must continue to do so. I don't doubt that you mean well, but I fear some things can never change."

Verity had nothing left to say. She nodded and wiped her eyes. The queen still did not look at her but moved to the edge of the room and pulled on a velvet cord. When a servant appeared, she spoke to him in a low voice. He dashed off, and in another minute, Sir Rufus joined them.

"Miss Grandin," said Lucerne softly. "I would like for you to go with Sir Rufus and explain to him what you have told me. See that he knows exactly where to—to *find* everything.

Sir Rufus, this young woman has done us a great service. She is to be treated with kindness and respect."

Verity understood. Her aching heart went numb. She would tell her story a second time. She would show Sir Rufus the secret panel and hidden tunnel. And he would see the boys' only source of joy and freedom undone.

She repeated the basics of her story to Rufus as they walked through the palace. He interrupted her with many remarks and exclamations, but the farther they walked, the less she noticed. She began to recognize rooms that she had passed through on the first night of her mission. Only now, the noonday sun poured through the windows from outside, making her feel exposed. Her hands trembled, and she glanced repeatedly over her shoulder, unable to kick the fear that she was being followed.

As they mounted the staircase that led to the royal family's private quarters, Sir Rufus finally caught on to her anxiety.

"Don't worry," he said. "We'll use the back hallway to get to the boys' bedrooms. No risk of any unpleasant *encounter* that way."

"Are you sure?"

"Quite. My younger nephews will have finished their lunch and returned to the schoolroom by now. I left Augustin on the other side of the palace. None of them shall stir from where they are until it's time for their afternoon exercise."

Despite this assurance, Verity thought she heard whispering, thought she saw movements from the corner of her eye. She continued casting backward glances but saw nothing.

Just my imagination playing cruel tricks, she told herself.

Verity thought she would feel easier once they had reached the eldest princes' room, but she did not. She hurried to move aside the bureau and show Sir Rufus how the secret panel behind it opened. Rufus didn't share her sense of urgency. He wished to examine every drawer in the bureau, along with its felted feet, and make meandering observations about everything. Once he got around to the hidden doorway, he was altogether engrossed. Verity stepped out of the way and left him to his investigative soliloquy.

"Remarkable!" Rufus said as he disappeared behind the panel. "Those clever rascals...I almost feel sorry for them. No, I *do* feel sorry for them. Six boys outwitted by a shoemaker's daughter."

Verity turned away from him, toward the open bedroom door, and froze.

Alexander and Christopher stood just outside the room, as paralyzed as she was. However much they had seen and heard, there was no question it had been enough. Sandy's face was wan as tallow. One of his hands rested on top of his head, fingers curled into his hair, as if he'd put it there and forgotten it. Christy looked like a youth who'd just had his heart broken for the first time. Verity's own heart crumbled as she realized that was just what he was.

Sir Rufus did not notice the boys as he ducked back into the bedroom. He mumbled minced oaths, preoccupied with the construction of the panel. Verity sucked in her breath, wanting to say something, *anything*, but not a syllable came out. Tears streamed down her cheeks. She turned to wipe them on her sleeves, and by the time she looked up again, the princes were gone.

Christy's mind spun out of control. What had just happened? He tried to think backward, to recall what had brought him to this moment.

He remembered lying to Mr. Hawk. An invented stomachache…an excuse to shirk his physics lesson for the afternoon. Of course, Mr. Hawk had only half bought it, and instead of an afternoon off, Christy had been sent to study in the library, which was quieter and boasted a new water closet next door. The more trustworthy Sandy was dispatched with him to make sure Mr. Hawk's instructions were carried out. It had still felt like a victory.

But then what?

Then everything had gone wrong. They had heard a familiar voice echoing through palace halls where it did not belong. They had followed it, spying Verity Bell with Uncle Rufus. Christy did not want to believe anything he had seen or heard after. But the testimony of his eyes and ears was beyond denial.

Sandy had pulled him away from the door of his bedroom and back toward the library, where they were supposed to be. At least, Christy assumed he had. They were in the library now, and he couldn't tell how else he would have gotten here.

His stomach really did ache now. Only it was nothing in comparison with the ache in his chest. His brain kept spitting out questions. Answers were in shorter supply.

"What are we going to do?" Sandy's whisper pushed through his own contemplations.

What were they going to do? He hadn't gotten as far as that question yet. But he welcomed it coming from his brother. They would have to tell the others, and then they *would* have to do something. The *what* questions might hurt, but not as much as the *why* ones did. And it was always better to be active than passive. There was one problem.

"I have no idea," Christy whispered back, hiding his face in his hands.

An hour passed before Christopher and Alexander were reunited with the rest of their brothers. Christy hadn't opened his mouth again the entire time. His thoughts and feelings continued in a sickening whirl. When they all convened in the courtyard for their afternoon exercise, the turmoil reflected in his eyes.

"Feeling better?" asked Goose with a snort.

"Something's wrong," Augie said when Christopher didn't react. "What is it? Are you actually sick?"

"We're both sick," Sandy lamented.

Christy beckoned to them, and they all huddled around him. Without once raising his voice above a whisper, he explained what had happened. They listened in stunned silence.

When all was known, Cassiel and Demetris had tears standing in their eyes. Alexander had hidden his face in his hands. Augustin looked like a ghost in attendance at its own wake.

"That conniving hussy!" Marcus said, slamming his fist against his open palm.

Christy admonished him gently. "Easy, Goose. It reflects more on you than on the girl, when you say things like that about her."

"Well, what are we going to do now?" demanded Marcus. "That's what I wanna know."

"We all knew this day would come," said a rueful Augustin. "There's nothing to do. We're finished."

Christy waved at them. "Shh! I'm still trying to think."

"Couldn't we—" Cal tried to say, but he had no actual ideas and his mouth hung open in helpless suspense.

Christy put an arm around him. The other encircled Goose, who was on his opposite side. "I've looked it over every which way."

His brothers all looked at him, feebly hopeful.

"And?" Sandy asked.

"And there's only one thing left that we can do."

CHAPTER NINETEEN

AFTER HER AUDIENCE with Verity Grandin, the queen had not left her study. She stayed seated behind her desk until the afternoon was spent. She did not so much as raise her head when a knock sounded at the door.

"Not now," she answered it. "I do not wish to be disturbed."

A hesitant voice responded. "Excuse me, Your Grace, but—"

"What is it?"

The door opened a crack, and a servant peeped through. "I do beg your pardon, Your Grace," she said. "It's the princes."

"What about them?"

"They request an audience, Your Grace."

The queen touched her chin and knit her brow, then waved her hand in the air. The servant shooed in all six princes, closing the door behind them. Lucerne stood up and looked at them one by one.

"Augustin," she said, "Christopher, Marcus. Alexander. Cassiel, Demetris. You surprise me. Why are you not at your studies?"

Christopher stepped forward, his face ashen. He swallowed before answering, but it didn't prevent his voice from cracking.

"Your Grace, we have something to tell you. We feel it's more important than our lessons, for the moment."

"Let me hear it, then."

The brothers exchanged looks of mingled reluctance and resolve.

Tris was crying. He moved next to Christopher and held on to his arm. "Our shoes are spoiled because we sneak out every night to play and have fun." The youngest prince sniffed.

"There's a hidden passage," Augustin added. "Out of our room. It leads outside."

One by one, the boys spoke up, piecing together their confession, leaving nothing out. Their mother listened in dazed silence.

"Please, Your Grace," said Christopher, when they had done. "Punish us how you will, but please don't do anything to the others—to our friends. We're the ones who did wrong, not them."

Lucerne looked at each of her boys in turn, ignoring Christopher's entreaty. She had scarcely heard it.

"You might have told me before," was all she said.

Then she sent them away again and did not join them for supper. Later that night, long after she had usually gone to bed, the queen remained wakeful, pacing the palace halls.

"Can I be of service, Your Grace?" asked the guard nearest her sons' rooms, as she wandered past him for the third time.

"No," she replied, then wavered. "Yes…I would like the keys to these doors."

The guard handed her the keys without question. She unlocked both doors before opening one and peering inside. The gentle, rhythmic breathing of sleeping boys floated through the dark. Lucerne listened until she began to feel sleepy herself. Then she eased the door shut, leaving it unlocked, and retreated to her own bed without returning the keys to the guard.

Christy and his brothers were left in suspense for three days. They saw their mother but once in that time, and she had not spoken a word about their indiscretions. The younger princes voiced a hope that perhaps she did not intend to punish them at all. The others were not so optimistic. They had reason to believe she'd been conducting extensive meetings with Uncle Rufus, along with their tutors, some of the household staff, and even a few complete strangers.

Though Christy had to admit he was sleeping better than he had in ages, his waking hours became an ever-increasing misery. The queen had something in store for all of them. She was taking her time to plan it. But what would it be? Stricter rules to follow? More guards to keep an eye on them? Perhaps she would conscript them into peeling potatoes in the kitchen or mucking stalls in her stable. Christy's greatest fear was that she would isolate them all from one another. He thought he could endure anything but that. Especially as he was still trying to process the deceptions of the girl he had admired so tenderly. Still, if the worst was to come, he wanted to get it over with.

Servants came to rouse the boys early on the third morning. Breakfast, for the time being, was to be skipped, and so were their lessons. The queen wanted to see them.

"Finally," Christy breathed.

"What do you think she's decided to do to us?" Goose wondered.

"She'll disinherit me," Augie said as he buttoned his shirt. "I'm sure of it."

"She will *not*," contested Christy. "She'd have to disinherit all of us, and who would she hand the crown to, then? Besides, you know she isn't going to do anything that might make this public."

Goose almost fell over trying to pull on a sock while standing up. "What, then?"

But Christy had no answer for him and neither did Augustin. Uncle Rufus appeared to escort them, along with the younger three, in a silent march to Lucerne's private chambers. When they arrived, her face was as inscrutable as ever. Christy stood as tall as he could. He took long looks at each of his brothers, as if it was the last time he was ever going to see them.

"Demetris?" the queen said, without so much as a *good morning.* "Cassiel?"

They stepped forward like little soldiers. "Yes, Your Grace?"

"Several men of great repute were lately my guests here in the palace. I am sure you have heard of Harold Chase and Frederick Merkle. They are known and respected throughout the city. And Charles Gandil is one of the most celebrated men of the age."

"Yes, Your Grace," they squeaked.

"I have been told that you snuck into their rooms. That you drugged their wine."

"We did, Your Grace."

To the boys' surprise, their mother did not reprimand them for these misdeeds. Instead, she asked to know exactly how they had been accomplished. What substance had been used? What manner of acrobatics had been undertaken to sneak it into the private chambers of her guests? Cal and Tris explained with quivering voices while Lucerne listened intently.

"I have spoken with a gentleman called Dr. Slaughter." The queen paused after she said this, allowing the boys time to imagine what horrible identity might belong to a person with such a name. "The doctor has an excellent reputation, and I trust him."

"Please don't send us away with him!" blurted Tris.

"Demetris!" his mother admonished.

He shut up.

"As I was saying, Dr. Slaughter is renowned throughout the country. He is one of the finest scientists we've ever called our own. Cassiel, are you listening?"

"Yes, Your Grace."

"I can arrange for you to apprentice with Dr. Slaughter, Cassiel. You would have to sacrifice your studies with Miss

Clement, and you would have to work hard. I have visited the doctor's laboratories, and he is a very particular sort of man. I am afraid he doesn't believe in books and tests. You would have to learn by watching and doing."

At first, Cal had looked confused. By the time Lucerne finished, his mouth hung open.

"A real laboratory?" he echoed, his fingers twitching. "With chemicals? And experiments?"

His mother remained cool. "Would you like that?"

He nodded violently and could do no more.

Christy, as he watched and listened, had fallen into a similar stupor. It was as if the queen had discovered the thing that would please Cal most and handed it to him in place of a punishment. As if he had approached the gallows for execution, only to be given the keys to the city instead. Was there a catch? Or were they in some kind of a dream?

Before any of them could begin to puzzle it out, Lucerne turned to her youngest with a handful of colorful pamphlets.

"I want you to look these over carefully, Demetris," she instructed. "I will talk to you again later, and you can tell me whether any of it looks appealing."

Tris gasped, his excitement triumphing over his confusion in an instant as he examined the pamphlets. They advertised lessons in fencing, archery, gymnastics, and a wide range of other athletics. They had lots of exclamation points and illustrations.

The queen turned to the four elder princes, who watched close-mouthed and wide-eyed.

"I have been treating you all as children," she said softly. "But you are not little boys anymore. It is time you were treated as young men. There will be changes in this house." She paused to look at her firstborn. "Augustin? You might not like all of them. You are my heir, and it is time you were given more responsibilities. It won't be easy, but I will do anything in my power to help you. I know what pressures, what uncertainty you must feel. I was a year younger than you, you know, when I inherited the crown."

"Yes, Your Grace."

"And Christopher? Do you know that I was your age when I married your father? You must learn alongside your brother, so that you can help him. I think it would benefit both of you to see a good deal more of the world. Travel is an education in and of itself."

She turned to Goose. He had passed her in height a year or so ago, but he looked childlike again when she put a hand on his shoulder.

"You are not forgotten, Marcus. I wonder if you will mind parting from your brothers to join me for lunch today."

"Just me?"

"Just you. We will talk of your future, as well as your present. And Alexander? Mr. Hawk believes you a prodigy beyond his range of expertise. I think it is time we tested such glowing assertions. I've been in touch with the finest music tutors in the country, and they are eager to meet you."

"Thank you, Your Grace!" cried Sandy. He could contrive nothing else to say. None of them could.

"That is all, for now," Lucerne said. "I imagine you're all ready for your breakfast—yes, Augustin! I heard your stomach growling."

Five boys shuffled out of the room in a dreamlike state. None of them noticed, and neither did the queen, when Christy lingered and closed the door behind them. He did not speak up right away but waited until his mother observed him.

"Christopher," she said, not unkindly. "I had hoped you'd be pleased, but you do not look it. Tell me what more I can do."

"I *am* pleased. Truly. It's just—one thing does still trouble me. May I have permission to ask you a question?"

She looked at him in a way he could not recall her ever having done before. Like she was just his mother and not his queen as well. "You need not ask permission."

"It's about the shoemaker's daughter."

"Miss Grandin."

Miss Grandin. Though his primary concern for the past few days had been his brothers, she had never been far from his thoughts. Now that he knew the boys would be all right, Verity Bell—no, *Grandin*—came crowding into his heart and mind.

"We know that you sent her to—well, to frustrate our escapades."

"She volunteered."

"Yes, and I want to know—if you know yourself, that is, Your Grace—why she did it."

The queen studied him closely, and for once, it did not make him squirm. "This is what troubles you?"

"Yes. See, she acted quite as a friend to all of us, and I—we all—feel like we've been double-crossed."

"Miss Grandin is a fine girl, Christopher, but I am very surprised, indeed, if you mean to suggest that she went out of her way to befriend you."

He flushed, started to say something, and had to start over. "I suppose it *was* more the other way around."

"So I thought."

"But she is a fine girl, as you said. And she looked so ill at ease, I couldn't help but be friendly to her. I hope it doesn't make you angry, Your Grace."

"No, Christopher. Miss Grandin herself told me of your kindheartedness. She's made me see it, too."

A tear stung the corner of Christy's eye. He blinked it away and took a deep breath. "What reward did you offer her? Was it so great?"

"She acted for the sake of her family, Christopher. Grandin was being run ragged, making shoes for you boys. He's been forced to turn away his other customers, even friends. He had to take his daughter out of school to help him. There was no joy in their home anymore, Miss Grandin told me. That was why she became my spy. Her reward was to have been nothing more than the cost of her education."

Christopher looked at his mother for as long as he could while she explained, but his head was soon hanging.

"I never— I'm glad—" he started to say, but could manage no more.

"It might also interest you to know that she would not have the reward, after all was said and done."

"What?"

"She would not accept it. It was a matter of conscience, she said. I thought it a terrible shame, but perhaps she may yet be persuaded. Do you think it possible?"

"Might be."

"Is that all you wanted?"

"Yes, thank you. I know how busy you are, Your Grace." He offered her a bow, more out of love than of deference, and started to leave.

"Christopher?"

He stopped and looked back.

"There is no need for you to address me that way. I am your mother. I think *Mother* will do very well from now on. You may tell your brothers."

It would be inaccurate to say that Christy loved his mother now more than he ever had before. He had always loved her. There is something distinct about the love between a mother and son. What is more, Lucerne was distinct from every other mother and Christopher from every other boy. Thus, it can well be said that no son ever loved his mother as Christy did his. And now, for the first time in his life, the door to this love had been unlocked. The key had been discarded. His heart was loosed, and such was his rapture that nothing would do but for him to go to the queen, put out his arms, and cling to her.

"Mother," he said, "I'm sorry we lied to you."

"Son," she whispered in reply, "I'm sorry I drove you to it."

CHAPTER TWENTY

ERITY STARED LISTLESSLY at her arms, which were submerged up to the elbow in soapy dishwater. Olive had the day off, so Verity was helping Nonna keep up with the housework. Downstairs, the shop bell burst out in its old merry tinkle. The sound made Verity smile for the first time in several days, though it was still a melancholic smile. The bell had begun to ring again. Life would soon return to normal.

Verity was glad, but she was not happy. She wasn't sure she could ever be happy again. Surely the dark memories of that ill-fated week would haunt her for the rest of her life. She sighed again, the smile gone and forgotten.

"Verity!" Nonna's voice dispelled her thoughts. "Verity! Come down to the shop. You're wanted right away!"

Verity wiped her wet, soapy hands on the front of her dress and passed quietly down the stairs. Stepping into the shop, the numbness she felt inside jumped suddenly outward. She stood as stiff and still as a lamppost, eyes wide and unblinking. Her heart quit beating for a moment, then resumed at double the pace.

Standing there amongst the lasts and leather was Prince Augustin. And beside him, Prince Marcus. Then Alexander and Cassiel and Demetris. At the end of the line, with his hands behind his back and a boyish simper on his face, stood Christopher.

Young Tris was the first to break ranks.

"Miss Bell!" he cried, stepping toward her. "We're out all by ourselves, without any governesses or anyone! And our mother let us! Isn't it the best, Miss Bell?"

"Her name isn't Bell, dummy," Cal hissed, slapping his younger brother, then looking back at Verity. "Miss *Grandin*," he said, "we've come to thank you."

Verity glanced to her left, where her father and Nonna looked on beaming, then back to the boys.

"You look a little boggled, Miss Grandin," noted Augie. "Maybe you thought we would be angry with you for spoiling our secret."

"Aren't you?" she asked.

"You changed everything, Miss Grandin," said Sandy.

"We much prefer having our mother to having dances," Marcus added. "I don't know what you said to her, but it worked wonders. D'you know what? She's even let us accept an invitation to a ball. We still get to dance!"

"And I get to apprentice with a real scientist!" said Cal. "He's going to let me mix chemicals and wear funny goggles and everything."

"I'm to learn gymnastics!" cried Tris with glee. "And mother is to let Sandy take lessons at the conservatory!"

"I can speak for myself," murmured Sandy.

"Christy and I are to travel, Miss Grandin," said Augie eagerly. "*Really* travel! All by ourselves. Uncle Rufus is to come along, of course, but I've never been so excited about anything! You see, Miss Grandin, how indebted we are to you. You've changed our lives."

Verity's heart had grown so much lighter as they spoke that she put her hand over her chest for fear it would float away.

"You're all happy?" she asked.

A chorus of smiles, nods, and yeses went up from the brothers.

"But—I lied to you."

"We forgive you, Miss Grandin." Christy spoke up for the first time. "With all our hearts."

Cal elbowed Tris, who pushed back. But then the youngest prince cleared his throat and approached Verity with as much gallantry as a ten-year-old could.

"Thank you, Miss Grandin," he said, bowing. He took her hand and kissed it before rejoining his brothers.

Cal came forward next and did the same. One by one, all the princes stepped up, thanked her, and kissed her hand. When it came to Christy, he took her hand like the others. But instead of bowing, he just held it and peered nervously into her eyes. Then, in one quick motion, he brushed his kiss upon her cheek instead. He turned away, blushing, while his brothers laughed, hooted, and clapped.

"My apologies, Mr. Grandin," he said, with a sheepish glance at the shoemaker. "They dared me to do it."

"I'll let it pass, just this once, Your Highness," returned the shoemaker sternly, but with a twinkle in his eye. "If my daughter will, that is."

"Forgive me, Miss Grandin," Christy said, in a lower voice, to Verity.

She did not say she forgave him...or curtsy...or anything. She could not. She was in a dream. The boys were filing back out the door a minute later, but Christy kept gazing at her to the last.

"Good-bye, Miss Grandin. We'll never forget you."

"Christy?" she was able to say, just before the door closed.

He looked back. "Hmm?"

"You can call me Verity."

He smiled at her one last time and was gone.

Epilogue

The day before she was to begin studies at her new school, Henry Louis Grandin Jr. had presented his daughter with the gift of a bicycle. Ridgewood was farther than she'd once had to travel, and the newfangled contraption would save her a lot of steps.

"Besides," he'd said, "the way you get around lately, I'm sure you'll find lots of other uses for it."

Verity had exclaimed against the idea. She'd had quite enough of the kind of *getting around* her father meant. She had accepted the gift gratefully, nonetheless.

She was riding down the street on her first day when she had a strange and sudden vision. She thought she saw, peeping at her from a street corner, a familiar face. It was tiny and round and toothless. It smiled, and she could have sworn it winked at her. But the next instant, it had vanished.

Verity shook her head, but she didn't spend too much time worrying over whether she was seeing things. It was her first day of school, after all, and she had no intention of being late.

GRATITUDE

TO MY PARENTS, grandparents, aunts, uncles, cousins, friends, and coworkers. This book would not exist in published form—or at all—without the lifetime of encouragement and support you have given me. I am sorry for lumping you all together like this, but to list each one of you individually would result in a tome of its own.

To anyone reading this who is unsure of whether or not they're part of the lump… you almost certainly are.

To the past and present members of the SVWCG, with special thanks to Miriam, Meg, and Allison for their feedback on this project.

To my editor extraordinaire, Arielle Bailey, for helping to hammer this story into shape, and spit shine it into its final glory.

To Deborah O'Carroll, for dotting the i's, crossing the t's, and death-glaring every last apostrophe into place.

To Timea at Fantastical Ink for the fittingly fantastical cover design.

To Savannah of Dragonpen Press for kicking things up a notch further with her beautiful interior formatting.

To Shelley Duval, who is largely to blame for my love of fairy-tales—the Dancing Princesses, in particular.

To all of the readers who made it this far. You might forget this story within a week, but I will love you forever.

Finally, to my own personal Author. All my thanks will never be enough.

ABOUT THE AUTHOR

ELIZABETH KIPPS is a lover of words and wonder who crafts stories for the young and young at heart. Small joys in her life include baking pies, addressing envelopes, and paying for things in exact change. She resides in the Shenandoah Valley of Virginia with a mischievous white cat and an inordinate number of bookshelves.

You can find more from Liz at www.ElizabethKipps.com